Rajam Krishnan
LAMPS IN THE WHIRLPOOL
(Suzhalil Mithakkum Deepangal)

Translated from the Tamil original by
UMA NARAYANAN & PREMA SEETHARAM

First Published 1995

MACMILLAN INDIA LIMITED
Madras   Jaipur   Patna   Vapi
Bangalore Bhopal Coimbatore Cuttack Guwahati
Hyderabad Lucknow Madurai Trivandrum Visakhapatnam
Associated companies throughout the world

SBN 033392 92 310 3

Typeset at Laserwords, Madras 600 020

Published by
Rajiv Beri for Macmillan India Limited,
21 Patullos Road, Madras 600 002 and printed by
V.N. Rao at Macmillan India Press, Madras-600 041

Whatever our quarrels and shifting factions, all Indians know that they have a complex, stable system of values, beliefs and practices which — though forged long ago — has never really been interrupted. It still underlines the surface differences and makes them comprehensible. Our programme of translations is an exploration of this Indian tradition which is one of humankind's most enduring attempts to create an order of existence that would make life both tolerable and meaningful.

The method we have adopted is to translate selections from the corpus of fiction Indians have created after their Independence (1947). It is our hope that these novels will express most of the ideas, customs, unquestioned assumptions and the persistent doubts that have characterised Indian life for at least a thousand years, and, more recently, after the impact of western ways of thinking on it.

Novels from Telugu, Tamil, Kannada, Malayalam, Gujarati, Oriya, Marathi, Punjabi, Urdu, Bengali and Hindi have been selected. We hope to include more Indian languages in the next phase.

This project has been made possible by the generosity of MR. AR. Educational Trust, of which Sri A.M.M. Arunachalam is the Trustee. Known to us, there has never been such a big and systematic programme of translations sponsored by the private sector.

Some of the footnotes may seem excessive, but they have been prepared with non-Indian readers in mind.

MINI KRISHNAN
Project Editor

INTRODUCTION

The novel *Lamps in the Whirlpool* is frontally feminist in its theme, treatment and language. The feminism that breathes through the story is an indigenous variety. It authentically stems from the writer's milieu and culture but raises issues which will find an echo in the hearts of many a repressed woman, cutting across culture and language. It asks the reader to ponder how we treat the woman in our society, woman who is the linchpin of the family, who effaces herself as a person so that she may be a wife, mother, daughter-in-law most of all. Virginia Woolf long ago wrote in *Professions for Women* about the Angel in the House:

> She was intensely charming. She was utterly unselfish. She excelled in the difficult arts of family life. She sacrificed herself daily. If there was chicken, she took the leg; if there was a draught she sat in it — in short she was so constituted that she never had a mind or wish of her own, but preferred to sympathize always with the minds and wishes of others. Above all — I need not say it — she was pure.

The Indian woman in the family is worshipped as an angel if she annihilates herself for the sake of others. Or else she is cast away as monstrous, if not demonic. Rajam Krishnan is so irate at the self-righteous middle/upper middle-class Brahmin community (the point of focus in this novel) that she dares to put its very citadel — the family — in a dubious light. In fact, she challenges through the central crisis of the story the legitimization of the atrocities perpetrated in the name of this institution.

She is unsparing in her criticism of the pretentious pieties of a family where there is no human consideration for the one woman who toils like a slave for its upkeep. This is a familiar subject but what gives an edge to Rajam Krishnan's treatment of it is the totally radical spirit she endows it with. There are no melodramatic dowry deaths or bride burnings, familiar feminist issues, especially in India, nor is there female infanticide, an issue which has moved Rajam Krishnan to profound creative anger in *Mannagathu Poonthuligal*. What we witness is the painful dawning of self-knowledge in the protagonist Girija, that she has been used like a draught animal by her mother-in-law and husband and that there is not even appreciation of her sincere service. Girija transforms into a new woman. Girija is a sort of Indian Nora.

How does this happen? To be sure Girija is not one of those activist women — she is a typical middle-class girl, educated only to be suitably married off to perform the duties of a Hindu wife in a Brahmin community. She has been trained to regard being a dutiful wife and daughter-in-law as the only goal of a woman's life. Although she is a post-graduate and has served in a village school near Chingleput in Tamil Nadu for eight years, inspiring her students and colleagues alike, she is given in marriage to Swaminathan ("Samu" as he is called in familiar circles) who is qualified and well placed in life. Swaminathan's mother — in fact she is as much a central character as Girija because she symbolizes the cruelty that (Indian) woman per- petrates on womanhood — having chosen Girija as a daughter- in-law calculates the prospect of her becoming a thoroughly obedient person. On the eve of the marriage she presents Gir- ija with a pair of diamond earrings and a pair of nosestuds. Such generosity is rare and Girija's mother and brother are deeply im- pressed. They do not expect anything to go wrong in Girija's life. After bearing two daughters and a son and serving her mother-in-law with uncompromising devotion for seventeen years observing strict rules of austerity and piety described by that one lethal Tamil word in the novel "madi" and its nefar- ious cousin "aacharam" (the two words and their debilitating impact on a woman will be presently discussed), Girija comes to realize the emptiness of her life and the insidious exploitation of her natural docility and goodness by the mother and son.

If the mother-in-law uses her daughter-in-law to maintain her own commitment to ritual piety and austerity, the husband is the embodiment of callousness so typical of many Indian husbands/men. He is not aware of his wife as a person at all.

The combination of a peculiar form of matriarchy and typical patriarchy is what chokes Girija's existence when she becomes aware of it, awakened by the talk of "consciousness raising" (to use a feminist term) by Ratna, her husband's niece, who is on a chance visit. While continuing to serve the family in simmering resentment, an incident which would appear almost utterly insignificant in our households, rouses the dormant sense of self-respect in Girija. After a long tour, Samu drops in only to pack up and leave on yet another professional trip. He is insensitive to his wife's state of mind. Losing his temper in wonted arrogance and unleashing male egoistic anger, he throws down the plate when the food is not to his liking and when he sees his wife somewhat sullen and uncommunicative. She is shocked by his crude behaviour and for the first time does not feel like apologizing. He humiliates her and goes away. His mother does not seem to think that her son was either unreasonable or boorish. (Much later in the novel she tells her daughter-in law such loss of temper in a man is nothing so odd as to make the wife take the drastic decision of leaving the family).

Girija leaves, hoping to get some relief from the oppressive atmosphere of the house by spending some time on the banks of the Ganga. She meets an elderly pilgrim couple and stays with them while in Haridwar. She finds that the old woman Gowri Ammal has been treated abominably by her arrogant husband who was a Munsiff. But in old age the woman talks of her past without any bitterness and ironically, now, her husband is totally dependant on her. Girija also meets a spiritual widow in Rishikesh who recounts her life of misery as third wife to an elderly man and the tale of tyranny of her stepson who was a menace to her youth. That woman finally dared to defy society after her husband's death by drowning while on a pilgrimage, and chose to stay in the Ashram at Rishikesh, helping a young sannyasin in his medical rounds in the neighbourhood as an Ayurvedic healer. Girija confesses to that woman about her situation and the latter asks her to take life in her hands and act with clarity. Girija feels enlightened and returns home after a gap of four days.

Quite naturally, the family and the neighbourhood are flabbergasted by Girija's flight for four days, leaving the old woman and the children untended. The mother-in-law and the husband charge her with infidelity and order her to clear out of the house. She is horrified by their cruel assumptions. What pains her more deeply is that Samu should have descended so low as to tell his son Bharat that Girija is a "loose" woman and has run away. Girija goes out in search of Ratna who is engaged in feminist research in Delhi University along with Abu (who early in the novel asks Girija pointed questions about what she has missed out on life after her marriage. That and Ratna's spirited talk against the old woman's vicarious practice of "madi aacharam" were what stirred discontent in Girija's mind). Understanding Girija's predicament, Ratna and her friends in the hostel give her temporary refuge and take care of her as if she were a wounded bird. Girija is torn between her worry for her daughters and her awareness that she must eke out a new life for herself. She fears that her daughters (Kavi and Charu) would be indoctrinated and regimented into the rigmarole of ritual piety. Now they are typical of the younger generation living in Delhi, with scant respect for any form of orthodoxy. But the son would be cherished with fondness because sons matter most in Indian families. The old woman goes over to the hostel accompanied by the servant Maya to hand over Girija's certificates and clothes but not her jewellery. What provokes Girija is a cheque for Rs. 10,000/- which Samu sends through his mother. Girija flings it back. Later she learns that her husband had also come up to the building but had preferred to stay in the car. She is now certain that there is no love lost between them. She pledges her gold chain in the bank (it was made out of her savings while working as a teacher before marriage) She seeks employment with a nun who is running a home for refugee children. Her concern now is to see that her daughters, when they grow up, are not destroyed by the family regimen.

The title of the novel is charged with feminist/reformist significance. The central image in the novel is the small leaf boat carrying an oil soaked wick sailing in the Ganga. Pilgrims set such leaf boats down on the river. Some boats succumb to the current; some do reach the shore far away. The tiny leaf boat with the burning wick symbolizes the fragile but courageous woman in our society trying to cope with its forces. The widow whom Girija meets in a Rishikesh Ashram is one such individual who has not only reached the shore but has succeeded in chalking out her life according to her conviction. She is the one who lights the lamp in the drifting Girija and steadies her.

The burning wick in the novel beckons many a woman in our society to act with vision. The Ganga and scenes around it have been brought in by the author at the heart of the novel and constitute its central positive network of imagery. The perennial hoary river has been sacred to the Hindus from time immemorial. It is a symbol of our cultural unity. Its water reminds us not only of the flow of life but its current warns us of the dangers as well. The holy places of Haridwar and Rishikesh, the plain and the higher reaches of the Himalayas, help connect the life of "samsara", the unbroken cycle of birth, death and birth again into this sorrowful world and the life of renunciation. Rishikesh is dotted with many monasteries/ashrams/hermitages that Girija had visited as a young girl. She now visits these places at the age of forty-six. She is able to comprehend the complexity of our lives. For in a crisis she seeks the Ganga not only for escape, but also for enlightenment which she receives in the encounter with the widow in Rishikesh.

If the lamp in the Ganga is at the centre of spiritual imagery, the network of rituals and observances designated as "madi" is at the centre of the novel's material imagery. The "madi", and "aacharam" constitute the social ideology of a Brahminical household. They are the apparatuses which control and determine the identity of the subject in the family. The word "madi" can be paraphrased rather than translated, for to translate it would amount to depriving it of its cultural force in the novel. By its very iteration all through the novel the word is able to recreate the atmosphere prevailing in orthodox Brahmin households. It is not anything dreadful or obnoxious but it can be used as a lethal instrument of torture of the members of the family although in itself it is an innocuous regimen of physical and ritual purity and cleanliness. It is a form of sheer drudgery entailing repeated baths in a day especially if rules of ritual purity are even involuntarily violated.

For example, the food is to be cooked by a person who strictly observes the austere rules. Should anyone not conforming to the rituals touch the food so cooked, its purity is deemed sullied, leading to a rather ridiculously abstract idea of pollution. It spares neither children nor adults. In short "madi" is an oppressively exclusive system for personal purity which can become obsessive.

The tragic thing about it is, it can alienate daughter from father or mother, daughter-in-law from parents-in-law and even from her own children. It can vitiate human relationship when primacy is given to external observances to the petrification of the spirit. Further it can also be a source of much hypocrisy as is tellingly portrayed in the character of Roja Mami, friend of the mother-in-law. Claiming to be more than a daughter through long contact, Roja Mami exploits the doggedness of the old woman for "madi" to kindle suspicion leading to inhumanity in the mother-in-law towards the helpless daughter-in-law. Girija discovers to her horror after her escapade in Haridwar that all that glitters is not gold. Roja Mami and her husband for all their performance of worship to the Pontiff ("Swamigal") camping at Haridwar, are really social culprits, amassing money and treasures illegally, hoarding part of them in her husband's steel almirah. (Samu refuses to disclose the truth of the antique box lurking in his bureau to Girija. His ties with Roja Mami seem to be more important than those with his wife). Roja Mami has no business to interfere in Girija's family affairs and set her husband and mother-in-law against her, pretending to preserve their "madi" and "aacharam". Girija in sheer rage lashes out at her: "You sanctimonious hag!! Your 'madi' and 'vizhuppu' are all sham, you smuggled gold, diamonds, evade taxes and use an ignorant old woman's house to stash away your ill-gotten gains. I don't want my children to become hypocrites, observing hollow 'madi' rituals". Of course such a denunciation shocks the husband and mother-in-law. But "with her flashing diamonds, outsized pottu, dyed black hair and gaudy silks", an appearance which sets off waves of revulsion in Girija, Roja Mami lies through her teeth that she did not see Girija at Haridwar though in all probability she did sight Girija in the crowd thronging around the Swamigal (Pontiff) while offering obeisance to him. Roja Mami lies in order to slander and malign an innocent woman. It is a pity that the old woman cares more for Roja Mami's offended self-respect than for her honest daughter-in-law's feelings simply because she believes Roja Mami is strict in observance of "madi" and that therefore her integrity is unimpeachable. The author shows what insidious harm "madi" does to human relationship. Through Girija, both when she punctiliously observes the ritual cleanliness in serving her mother-in-law and when she is aghast at being ostracized, the author castigates the system of "madi" and its observances and their allied virtues. Not only that, Rajam Krishnan shows the unforeseen ramifications of the system.

What are the feminist issues this novel raises? It examines the changing values of a society and their impact on women in Indian families. The modern woman is at the cross-roads and she has to choose if she is not to end up with regrets for the road not taken. Although specifically the novel touches on the Brahminical milieu and its orthodoxy which is not a jot diluted for all its being located in the country's elite and cosmopolitan capital, the novel evokes the image of the Indian woman and her plight caught up in obligations towards her family. The most pathetic aspect of her situation is that she almost loses her sense of self. Her personality simply does not exist any more after her marriage. Education has not given her any rationale of her life. She becomes a sacrificial goat in the rituals of running the family. There is no time for her for "atma-vichara", self-inquiry. She loses hold of the fact that she is an entity and has a responsibility to herself and the society. When an educated woman is sunk in such torpor, society suffers more because the possibilities of her enlightening its members become remote. Rajam Krishnan has been fired by the rage for reform all through her career and in this novel too, she asks us not to think atomistically but of the society as a whole in our capacity as its citizens. If some of our institutions have been fostered at the cost of simple humanity and enlightened behaviour, then such institutions deserve to be divested of their sanctity. Hence the exit of Girija from her family. When the sacred turns sanctimonious then it is time we exposed it. Rajam Krishnan, to be sure, is not promoting subversion of the institution of family for the sake of revolt but she uses it as a shock-treatment to impel us to think about the essentials of human relationships. Crusted over by custom, debilitated by rituals like "madi", our present-day family is a far cry from its ideal. Girija does not reject it in a facile spirit of rebellion. She is, in fact, agonized by the choice she has to make of giving up her children. For, to the Indian woman, even to an adultress, motherhood cannot be compromised under any circumstance. In fact, it is true even to say that patriarchy has indoctrinated both men and woman to regard motherhood as inviolably sacred. The author would much rather have her New Woman think rationally and dispassionately about her duties to her children. That is why at the end of this novel, the mother in Girija resolves that she will keep in touch with her daughters and train their sensibility in a balanced way, giving them freedom while helping them to develop a sense of self-reliance and responsibility — in short to choose between freedom and licentiousness. Those will be the true alternatives, not freedom and submission which ensures security and protection.

The novel looks at gender discrimination with resentment. The conditioning of Girija's mind both before and after her marriage is eloquent testimony to the dangers of the existing norms of gender in our society. The double standards with regard to chastity which make Samu and his mother arraign innocent Girija on her absence from home for four days are a target for the author in her criticism of patriarchy. In fact, patriarchy, as Kate Millett convincingly demonstrated in *Sexual Politics* is complicit with power and power circumscribes woman at the biological, psychological, sociological and legal levels. That is why Samu has the audacity to expect Girija to be mute like an animal and throw her out when she at first demurs, then defies him. The new woman, the Indian Nora, emerges in the face of such a patriarchal assertion of power. Rajam Krishnan does not present her advent in a glib way. There are varieties of new women that this short novel sketches. Ratna, of course, is the most articulate. It is she who stirs the fearless self in her aunt Girija. She reminds Girija of her earlier vivacity and good work as a teacher. Ratna is naturally looked upon as the very devil sowing the seeds of discord in an otherwise peaceful family. She does not care about this. She researches in women's studies and she boldly believes in calling a spade a spade. But she is also aware that the new women like Runo in the hostel who commits suicide unable to face the challenges of her altered life, need balance. "On the one hand your 'mami-yar' with her 'madi' rules", she tells Girija, "and on the other, Runo with no rules". The implication is the question on how the Indian woman should learn to strike a balance between two extremes. The word "mamiyar" symbolizes authority which is often associated with inhumanity. The power wielded by the mother-in-law radiates every time the word "mamiyar" appears in the course of the novel. But at the end one ponders, what is the use of power without culture and education? In fact the sight of her mother-in-law in widow's weeds and tonsured head only evokes pity in Girija's mind. Girija has compassion. She is even willing to extenuate the harshness of her mother-in-law on account of her ignorance. But the author is unwilling to let go easily the ignorance in women. Rajam Krishnan, like an Old Testament prophet, is severe on sin. She does not spare even her pathetic heroine when the latter is entrenched in old-world thinking. For example, Girija worries that she has jumped from the frying pan into the fire when she suspects that the liberated girls in the hostel have undesirable habits such as smoking and using drugs. When she finds out that the white object in the ash tray in Ratna's room is not a cigarette stub but a half-burnt sandalwood incense cone (which itself was of inferior quality), she becomes contrite that she judged them wrongly.

Rajam Krishnan presents her society in a state of transition, especially in its treatment of women. For those caught in this condition, life is not going to be easy. But the author makes her protagonist train herself to face it, for the struggle lies ahead and is not over.

C.T. INDRA

ONE

Girija packed the filter with ground coffee and poured boiling water over it. Placing a cheese and peas filling between two slices of buttered bread, she slid it into the sandwich toaster. A tantalizing aroma filled the air as she grilled the sandwich over the fire.

Charu called out from the kitchen door: "Amma[1], the jamedarini[2], Vandana, is here. Wow! Give me some of the filling!". Though fully aware that touching the filling would pollute it, she grabbed a handful and dashed off to the terrace.

"Che! She hasn't even brushed her teeth this morning," muttered Girija.

Twelve year old Charu was totally irresponsible and interested only in food. She was gaining weight steadily and looked unattractive.

"You donkey! Stop looking at the sparrows and open the door for Vandana! Let her come in by the side door and take the rubbish away."

"Patti is awake and sitting up in her room," Charu alerted her mother.

Patti was the children's grandmother and Girija's mother-in-law — her Mamiyar. Her room opened out onto the terrace.

Mamiyar had decreed that the rubbish bin referred to as the "kacchada dabba" should not be allowed inside the house, since it was a receptacle for the remains of meals, like fruit peel, leftovers from plates and curry leaves, all considered "polluted" by the orthodox. Although it was a hygienically covered pedal bin it had been assigned a place in a far corner of the terrace. Moreover, it was the job of the sweeper Vandana, to remove the rubbish, and obviously she could not be allowed to enter the house.

---

[1] mother
[2] a common term used in North India to refer to the low-caste sweeper woman who removes garbage and cleans toilets.

It annoyed Vandana to be addressed as "jamedarini", the sweeper woman. "Call me by name," she would demand, justifiably, for after all, she did not look like a sweeper.

Dressed in a spotlessly clean and colourful salwar-kameez with glistening red kumkumam[1] on her forehead and neatly combed hair, Vandana looked as fresh as a newly blossomed flower. She took care to leave her sandals outside and came in with long, confident strides.

Vandana emptied the rubbish from the bin into the bucket in her hand and swilled the bin thoroughly with water that Girija poured out for her, lined it with paper, and left the house, bucket and broom in hand.

It was already half past six. Girija's elder daughter Kavita had still not got up. She was in class ten and had to leave for school by half past seven.

"Charu, wake Kavi. Every day she asks to be woken up at five and again at half past five. She never gets up, though."

The servant woman, Maya, who belonged to a higher caste than Vandana, was allowed to enter certain parts of the house. However, since she came only at nine, Girija had to clean the area that Vandana's presence had defiled, while Mamiyar kept a close watch.

Resentment stabbed Girija as she swept and mopped the floor.

Had Vandana been allowed to enter the house, she would have cleaned the wash basin and bathroom and left them sparkling. However Mamiyar had delegated this chore to Girija, adding to her already heavy morning schedule. Two different meals had to be prepared; first, one for her husband and children and after another bath, the second, a madi[2] meal for her Mamiyar. The children's father had gone abroad and was expected back the next week, which meant that Girija had a short respite from her rushed routine. The leftovers of yesterday's kuzhambu[3] and kootu[4] taken from the refrigerator and heated up would do nicely for the children to eat now with freshly

---

[1] a paste or powder worn as a decorative or auspicious mark.

[2] ritual purity; see introduction.

[3] a South Indian curry.

[4] a mix of lentils and vegetables.

cooked rice. Toasted sandwiches with a filling of cheese and peas had been packed in lunch boxes, ready to take to school.

Nine year old Bharath, the baby of the family, always had to be hugged by his mother as soon as he woke up. His school was nearby.

"Amma, my teacher has asked me to bring a box of coloured crayons."

"Why didn't you tell me earlier? Where's the one I bought you last week?"

"Charu took it from me and broke it."

"Liar! Liar! He broke my geometry box and doesn't want you to know."

These last minute squabbles just before they left for school were routine. The moment the children left and peace prevailed, it was a signal for Mamiyar to come out and begin her morning ablutions.

Since Delhi is the capital city, most houses and flats were for government servants. The company paid a rent of a neat three thousand five hundred rupees for this first floor flat with its three bedrooms and two bathrooms. Samu's position in the corporate ladder entitled him to a flat and other amenities. And yet....

A quick survey after the girls left revealed Kavita's clothes strewn all over Mamiyar's bathroom. The lazy girl had probably not had a bath at all. She would bathe in the evening or at night... Couldn't she at least have flushed the toilet?

Annoyed and disgusted, Girija cleaned the bathroom.

She switched on the geyser for Mamiyar who took at least forty-five minutes to complete her lengthy ablutions.

Girija started to get the youngest ready for school. Bharath had to be coaxed to eat in the mornings. Pampered by his father and grandmother, he always insisted that his mother feed him. Girija performed the daily ritual of carrying his school bag down the stairs and waving to him till he reached the corner of the street, where the school bus picked him up.

Girija went upstairs again. Her next job was to mop the floor in front of Mamiyar's array of deities and decorate it with a kolam[1]. The owner of the flat, Malhotra, a widower in his

---

[1] designs drawn with wet or dry rice powder signifying the cosmic pattern.

seventies, who lived downstairs, picked jasmine, mandarai and a few hibiscus flowers from the front garden for Mamiyar's puja. He had great respect for her puja rituals. He lived in a joint family with his three sons and their wives.

His daughters-in-law fussed over him a great deal. Two cars, an Ambassador and a Maruti, both protected by tarpaulins, blocked the driveway completely and bore witness to the family's affluence. In addition, three two-wheelers, one for each of his sons, stood in single file. A Nepalese boy cooked for them and did the dusting. The maid, Nirupa, would come only after eight o' clock to do the cleaning and washing.

When Girija gathered up the children's clothes and took them to the tap, she saw the second daughter-in-law, dressed in a housecoat, engrossed in painting her nails in the courtyard below. Her only son was away at Doon School.[1]

"Good morning auntiji."

"Good morning", replied Girija. She found it difficult to smile.

Surely, Girija thought, this girl was not young enough to address her as 'aunty'. All the Malhotra women belonged to a culture which aped the superficialities of western ways: short hair, lavish make up, brilliant red lips and nails, not to mention the seductive, flimsy saris which revealed more than they hid. But not one of them had completed her college education. No one would ever know from Girija's drab appearance that she was an M.A., B.Ed.

The truth was not that Girija did not have the time to look at herself in a mirror, but that she did not have the desire and enthusiasm to do so.

Her madi clothes, along with Mamiyar's narmadi[2] sari, were drying on the long clothes line in the passage, which was why Vandana could not come in that way.

She took her madi sari and pavadai[3] from the clothesline, using a madikol[4] and left them outside.

---

[1] an exclusive public school in India.

[2] silk-like cloth woven of fibres of certain plants, made into a nine yard sari, which a Brahmin widow wears, drawing the loose end over her shaven head. It is dull beige in colour with a fine ochre or red border.

[3] an ankle length skirt.

[4] the thin bamboo pole used to remove madi clothes from the clothes-line. The madikol is a common sight in Brahmin households.

She bathed, and still dripping wound her madi sari around herself and wrapped the madi towel around her wet hair. She then took her Mamiyar's dry madi sari and went towards the bathroom door when....

Girija suddenly realised that she had forgotten to put kumku-mam on her forehead.

She took a peek into the mirror, quickly took a little kumku-mam on her finger and placed a pottu[1] on her forehead. She was ravenously hungry, which in turn made her feel edgy.

If only she could stretch out in a chair, munch a freshly toasted, crisp cheese filled sandwich and slowly sip a mug of steaming coffee.... Her thoughts were interrupted.

"Giri, can you bring my sari?"

"Coming, Amma."

She handed Mamiyar the towel and sari on the tip of the madikol, through the partly opened bathroom door.

The sagging breasts, the folds of a stomach outlined by a clinging wet sari, the stubble of white hair on her head: the figure inside the bathroom stirred a familiar feeling of pity in Girija.

A flash of rage smothered her pity when she remembered that this woman had treated her like a worm for the past seventeen years.

Wrapping the sari around her, Mamiyar slowly came out of the bathroom. The viboothi[2] container and a metal chembu[3] with madi water were placed near the cupboard which held the deities.

"Has the child gone to school?"

"Mm...."

"He was coughing all night. Did you give him any medicine?"

"Hm..."

"Light the lamp before you go. It is Krithigai[4] today, why don't you make a little payasam[5]?"

---

[1] the vermillion dot Hindu women wear on their foreheads.
[2] sacred ash.
[3] a small brass container.
[4] an auspicious star/day because it is Lord Muruga's star.
[5] sweetened rice and milk spiced with cardamom.

Two

The servant maid Maya rang the door bell. Maya was not allowed into the kitchen. She could not use the kitchen sink in which vessels were normally washed. So, on Mamiyar's insistence, an additional sink with a tap had been provided in a small verandah-like space outside. The rent had, of course, been immediately raised from three thousand to three thousand five hundred rupees.

Madi rules being inflexible, vessels washed by Maya had to be rinsed before Girija could take them in. Maya's job was to wash the children's clothes and dry them on the terrace. She gathered and folded them at four in the afternoon. She took the school uniforms with her and brought them back, neatly pressed.

Under no circumstance was Girija allowed to touch the children's clothes and non-madi material like curtains and sofa covers. Nor was she permitted to have physical contact with her daughters before she served her Mamiyar the evening meal. However, these constraints did not apply to Bharath. Girija could touch any uncovered part of his body as long as their clothes did not come in contact. Sons and unwashed new silk do not pollute, goes the saying.

"Didiji[1], I can't come this evening," said Maya while she scrubbed the vessels.

"Why?"

"My child is not well, Didiji. I have to take him to a doctor."

"What is wrong with him? I saw him play with a stray dog yesterday. I have told you over and over again not to let him touch dogs. The dog may be mangy."

"Oh, Didiji, he doesn't listen to me! He had fever all night. I need a rupee to get a place in the queue at the doctor's."

Giving her the rupee was not a burden. If Maya did not come in the afternoon to fold the clothes, it would be left to

[1] a term of respect for the young women of the house, meaning "sister".

her to rinse the clothes washed by Maya, hang them to dry, and then bathe before cooking lunch for Mamiyar.

She bolted the door when Maya left. She made the rice and dal[1] in the cooker for the madi meal. Mamiyar had told her to make payasam, to offer as naivedyam, the votive offering of food for the Gods.

As Mamiyar concluded japam[2] and parayanam[3] and as the naivedyam was being offered, the door bell rang.

Who could it be?

Girija opened the front door. She saw a tall slim woman, without a single ounce of spare flesh on her body. She was smartly dressed and her hair was back combed and fluffed out.

"Giri, don't you recognise me? ...I am Kalpana's sister, Ratna, your Mamiyar's granddaughter."

Girija smiled uncertainly. "Oh! you've lost so much weight. I couldn't recognize you. And, you've done something to your hair too. Come in...come in..."

"I am coming in anyway, whether you invite me in or not."

Ratna laid a friendly hand on Girija's shoulder. When Girija shrank away she teased, "Are you afraid you will violate Mamiyar's madi rules? My patti is a difficult Mamiyar, isn't she?"

Ratna put her case down in the drawing room. She seemed overawed by the carpets, the decorative pieces in the corners, the batik wall hanging and the crystal chandeliers.

"Wow! Fantastic! Kalpana gave me your address. She told me she visited you when she came to Delhi on office work two months ago.."

"Yes, she rang up one day...Chittappa[4] invited her and her family for dinner. I believe her husband is back from Saudi Arabia and wants to set up an industry here."

"Their marriage seems to be shaky .... He nags her all the time 'You wear kumkumam and visit temples,' he says, 'it will be difficult for our son to find a bride in my community if you behave like this.' She has a good job and could easily leave him. She doesn't need his money, after all. She doesn't talk

---

[1] lentils.
[2] a silent recitation of mantras.
[3] the ceremonial recitation of sacred texts.
[4] father's younger brother.

about it, but she is deeply disturbed. Men are such rogues, such rascals. Imagine, he's singing a different tune after fifteen years of marriage. Now that he's so well off, he has become very arrogant. He is less educated than she is. He is only a mechanic. Now he insists that she cover her head and change her name..."

Giri said nothing. Ratna's older sister Kalpana who was a year her junior in college had been a frequent visitor to their house. Both Girija and Kalpana were fatherless. Four years after they had last met, the two girls and their mothers ran into each other accidentally in a temple. Girija's marriage was a natural consequence of that chance encounter.

Kalpana's father and Girija's husband Samu were stepbrothers. Kalpana's father had demanded his share of the ancestral property and had squandered it on drink. Soon after the partition of their property, he had moved to Bangalore and had not kept in touch with the family. His health had deteriorated progressively and he had fallen ill and died. Kalpana's mother had learnt to tailor clothes and had managed to educate her two daughters.

"What are you doing now?"

"I did my Master's in Sociology and am working for my Ph.D. My guide is at the university here. I have to stay in Delhi for a few days and do my field work. I suppose Samu is still at the office."

"He has gone to Japan and will be back on Wednesday."

"I arrived yesterday. I stayed with a cousin of my mother's in Karol Bagh. Poor things! They live in a tiny barsati[1], so I decided to move here."

"Come in, you can share the children's room."

Once she was in madi clothes, Giri was not allowed to enter the room. She had to pick up the children's clothes and tidy the room before she had a bath. The spacious room had three cots, open book shelves and a big writing table. The table and the cots were littered with cassettes. Over the thick layer of dust that covered the radiogram lay an assortment of things: a small bottle of shandu[2], books, crochet hooks...

---

[1] enclosed space on the terrace of a house.
[2] black or red pigment used as a pottu.

"I have to serve Patti her food, Ratna. Would you like to have a bath? Please use this bathroom."

"Ah! So you are still terrified of Patti! Does she continue to harass you with her madi?"

"Don't ask questions. If she finds out I have entered this room, she will refuse to eat."

"Let her starve! Why do you let her intimidate you?"

The words stirred up the discontent which had long been buried in the recesses of her heart.

"Doesn't Chittappa say anything?"

"Hm... that's the whole point."

"Male chauvinism! They trample on us, because we are far too soft." Giri turned away without a word.

After finishing her puja, Mamiyar sat staring into space with a scowl on her face, waiting to be served her meal.

"Who is that?"

"Ratna."

With a look of pure venom, Mamiyar pulled her sari tightly over her head: a sure sign of anger!

"So you were talking to her all this time! What brings that creature here? Her elder sister had the gall to marry out of the community. Whom has the younger one found? Obnoxious girls! We have our daughters to consider. Why should they associate with those girls? Look at Kalpana! A fine marriage indeed, without a thali[1] or nose ring."

How would Mamiyar react if she knew that Ratna had come to stay? Why am I afraid? Don't I have rights in my own house?

Silently, she placed a plantain leaf before Mamiyar, along with a glass of warm water to drink.

It was Krithigai, so she served payasam in addition to rice, dal, ghee, curds, brinjal thuvayal[2], rasam[3], green plantain poriyal[4] ...

Ratna emerged fresh from her bath, wearing a flowered kaftan. She was glad to have got rid of the grime of train travel. She carried the clothes she had washed.

---

[1] a gold pendant, the symbol of marriage, strung on a chain. Worn by women.
[2] egg plant roasted and mashed.
[3] watery, spicy soup with lentil or tamarind base.
[4] chopped fried and seasoned vegetables.

She hung her salwar, kameez, pavadai, undergarments and sari on the clothes line on the terrace. She rubbed her wet hair with a towel till it was dry and in separate strands. The scent of shampoo wafted across in the breeze.

"Is this your own house, Giri?"

"No, it is rented. We pay three thousand five hundred per month".

"Oh, I suppose the company pays. Has Patti finished lunch?"

"Yes, come. You can have yours now."

Giri brought out a porcelain plate reserved for visitors, placed it on the table and started to serve.

"How about you?"

"You eat first. I'll eat after I serve you."

"Why? Isn't there enough rice in the cooker for both of us? Make some more. We'll eat together."

"Oh no!"

Ratna ignored Giri's protests and marched straight into the kitchen. She lifted up the lids of all the vessels, including those that contained the madi meal. She picked up a plate and placed it on the dining table. Without washing her hands she opened the refrigerator, took out a bottle of cold water, then the pickles and the curds.

"Ah! what pickle is this?"

"Nellikkai[1]. Sit down, I'll serve you."

"I won't hear of it. Why can't we eat together? Has your Mamiyar forbidden you to eat with me, because my sister has married out of the community?"

Suddenly Girija was afraid. The hatred and resentment that she had nursed for a long time threatened to explode now.

Ratna went on, "Why are you so stubborn? You always make sure that everyone has eaten before you sit down on the floor of this dreary kitchen. Are you no better than a four legged creature that you only eat leftovers? Where is the old Girija, with all her degrees, a Master's and a B.Ed, who taught in school for eight years? Why are you terrified of this hag with her shaven head? Can't you reason for yourself? Oh...come on...Giri."

---

[1] gooseberry.

Had anyone ever shown such genuine concern for her? Her Mamiyar, her husband, even her own children?

She had duties to fulfill towards all of them. Each time she had a baby, her mother had stayed with her a mere twenty two days. After that, she had learnt to cope on her own, to look after herself and the child, and to resume charge of the household two months after the baby was born.

Her husband had worked in Madras when their two daughters were small. Kavi and Charu ran naked like slum children. If they wore clothes and touched her, she had to bathe again before cooking! She had been so ashamed of their appearance, especially when friends and students visited her.

As time passed, she taught her daughters not to touch her if they were clothed, especially after she had her bath. So they were denied the joys of being caressed and fondled by their mother from a tender age. The rule had been slackened, however, for Bharath. Since he was a boy, he could touch her, but not her clothes. And if the rule was accidentally broken, all was forgiven: he was a boy after all!

"The nellikkai pickle is out of this world." Ratna looked at Giri. "Giri, what's the matter? Why are you crying? Stop it!"

Embarassed, Giri wiped her eyes. She pulled the plate towards her and they began to eat.

"You are an excellent cook, Giri. The sambar and the cheese and peas curry are delicious. What is the secret?"

"Nothing but onions and peas."

Giri struggled with a sharp sense of guilt. What if Mamiyar found her eating at the table with Ratna? It was against the rules for Giri to eat at the table.

Ratna mixed rice and thuvayal with her right hand and then used the same hand to help herself to sambar and ate slowly, savouring each mouthful.

"It's years since I ate like this. The sambar-thuvayal combination is yummy."

Her praise was very sincere. Giri finished her meal in five minutes and sat and watched Ratna eat, fascinated by her guilelessness. She felt that Ratna had the courage to face life and accept its challenges boldly. She wondered why she was such a coward. Why did she shrink into herself when confronted with problems?

Ratna finished everything on her plate, then licked her fingers with relish.

"Can I serve you some curd and rice?"

"Oh no! I am full, Giri. Can't eat any more."

"There is payasam also," said Giri.

"What a feast! I'll have some in a small bowl".

Giri also helped herself to some payasam.

"Tell me Giri, you are imprisoned in the four dark walls of this tiny kitchen where your education and skills are wasted. Giri, are you happy with this life?"

Tears filled Giri's eyes again. Why did Ratna have to twist a knife in her wound?

"It makes me mad to look at that old creature. She had her head shaved only because she wanted to be admitted into Swamigal's[1] presence. I can't understand her reasoning. After all, at the time Grandfather died, this harsh custom was on the wane and my father forbade it. I was a child and did not understand, but I learnt later that it was this interfering old woman who turned my grandfather against my parents. Of course, my father was also to blame. Patti is a real schemer. I have never seen her smile. For us, Patti has always meant...'keep away'...'don't touch!'"

"Why rake up all those old stories? Get up and wash your hands...!"

"My hands can wait. I cannot bear to see a talented person like you trapped in a life ruled by blind orthodoxy. The madi concept is quite outdated and is only a means to torture people. Patti's son travels a lot. Don't tell me he never touches beef or pork! What justice is there in bullying you?"

A stab of bitter-sweet emotion brought tears to Giri's eyes. She flicked them away. She wanted to hug Ratna. Ratna's overture of friendship had made her sharply aware of her own sense of isolation and of the fact that she was trapped in a dessicated existence dominated by the madi routine.

"Ratna, don't shout...She may hear...Why provoke a scene?"

[1] a religious leader/teacher.

"I hope she hears. If your Mamiyar were an intellectual or a person concerned with social issues, it would be your duty to serve her, but even then, only if you could retain your self respect. You are not her daughter by birth. You are not her slave just because you married her son. My mother remembers visiting you in Madras. She said your daughters were wearing woollens totally unsuited to the climate, because they had sore throats from running naked in the rain. All because wool was madi. My mother was appalled. People like you are an anachronism."

"Things have been much better since we came to Delhi. At least there are no restrictions as far as Bharath is concerned."

"Do you believe Bharath is going to stand by you? Giri, doesn't Chittappa understand?"

"Aiyo! The day we got married he made his views clear by saying, 'My mother is old, you will have to do exactly what she wants for the few remaining years of her life'."

"Ha...a few years indeed! She will live to be a hundred. You'll never outlive her, she will wear you out. Doesn't her son realise what is happening? I am going to confront him when he returns."

"Ratna, please don't make things awkward for me. Domestic harmony is my first priority."

"What a disgrace! They treat you like a worm and make you work like a machine. Harmony is achieved only when all the notes are in perfect accord. A single note, however melodious, does not create harmony."

Having made her point, Ratna left the room.

THREE

Giri slid thenkozhal[1] into the smoking oil. It was three o' clock in the afternoon. The wet grinder was out of order. She had not had time to send for the electrician.

---

[1] a savoury made of rice and lentil dough deep fried in oil.

Ratna got up after her nap and began to fold the clothes in the verandah. A whiff of foreign perfume announced Roja Mami's arrival.

Giri came out of the kitchen, went through the dining room and stood at the door to the terrace, from where she could see Mamiyar's room. She could clearly see a flash of red silk. Roja Mami usually went up the stairs straight to Mamiyar's room. She never rang the bell, never came through the main door.

Girija heard Roja Mami complaining, "We wasted three holidays. We had an unending stream of visitors. My husband refused to take me to see Swamigal. Perhaps next week......"

To which Mamiyar replied, "I also want to have a darshan[1]. But we can't, unless we are destined to. Things rarely happen the way we want them to."

"You don't have to worry. Once Samu comes, he'll take you by car. Or, you can come with us."

Mamiyar's tone was affectionate. "You are more than a daughter to me, Roja."

"That's only natural, after all I look upon you as my mother. Only the lucky ones are given a chance to look after old people. I have brought wheat halwa[2] specially for you. I made the khoya[3] at home from fresh milk. Others would have bought the khoya and paneer[4] from the shop, but I know you won't eat anything from a shop."

Mamiyar helped herself to the sweet.

"You can do ten different things with your ten fingers if you want to, Roja. The halwa is like ambrosia."

Giri could not bear to listen a moment longer to the exchange of compliments. She entered Mamiyar's room. "So, Mami when did you come? You come only to see Patti."

"You seem to have a visitor."

Ratna came in, her hands piled with folded clothes.

"How are you Patti? I am Ratna, your grand daughter."

---

[1] a formal glimpse of a deity or an exalted person.
[2] a sweet dish.
[3] thickened milk.
[4] cottage cheese.

Patti examined her from top to toe. Then she pulled her sari tightly over her shaven head.

"You took your time to come and ask how I am! What brings you here?

"I have come to stay for a few days. Is that all right Patti?"

"I am sure your aunt will enjoy fussing over you. Why ask me? Is this my house? I don't want to be in anyone's way, so I remain quietly in my corner."

"Ayyayyo! Why should you remain in a corner? You are a queen, reigning over her domain."

"Sweet words from a forked tongue! Did you hear what she said, Roja? Am I a queen?" She turned to Ratna. "Are you quoting your mother's words? How long did she suffer my reign, may I ask?"

"Leave my mother out of this."

Feeling the tension, Giri quietly slipped away.

"Poor Chitti! Look how frightened she is of you."

"Don't be silly! Why should she be afraid of me? Don't underestimate her. She is a deep one. She pretends to be docile in my presence. As for my poor son, he never has a moment's rest. His job takes him all over and he eats and sleeps when and where he can. Besides, housework is no longer the drudgery it used to be. Electricity, gas, pressure cookers, heaters in winter, coolers in summer: what more can one desire?"

Roja Mami put in her bit. "No wonder she has time to sleep in the afternoon. She complains that I don't go into the drawing room. Every visitor uses the sofa. How can I sit on the sofa after it has been polluted by all sorts of people sitting on it? Even at home, I use a plain cane chair without upholstery like the one in this room."

Mamiyar launched a tirade: "Two daughters. As for Kavi, she has already come of age, and is still so innocent. She argues with me all the time. It upsets me. The price of gold and diamonds is soaring. We have to make enough jewellery and get them married at the appropriate time. Now, take Ratna's sister, she married most unsuitably and brought disgrace to the family. As for this one, she is already thirty. She does what she pleases. Why am I fated to see all this? None of them respect our customs. No one follows the rules of madi and purity in this house. No wonder the world is full of sickness! Bharath is hardly nine and has to wear glasses. It's all because they don't observe madi." The old woman tightened the sari over her shaven head in disgust.

When the children returned from school, Girija was busy rolling out puris[1] for Patti. The girls were delighted to see Ratna. They switched on the cassette player in their room and played western pop music which Girija detested. The children jumped up and down in glee, keeping time with the throb of the drumbeats.

"What's for tiffin?"[2]

"Puris, then thenkozhal..."

"What a bore. Why didn't you make vegetable puffs?"

"I used up all the peas for the sandwich filling. I'll soak the puris in milk."

"No. We don't want puris."

The children did not eat. All they had was coffee. Ratna took them out a little later.

Mamiyar usually had her night meal by six. Girija took her puris soaked in milk. The old woman had had a wash, smeared viboothi on her forehead and was seated staring vacantly out of the window.

"Amma...I've brought puris for you"

"I don't want them.."

She turned her face away dismissively. Girija was infuriated. She swallowed hard to control her anger and asked, "Why?"

"Don't pester me with whys. Can't I miss a meal if I want to? How I wish I could cook for myself. Then you would not have to ply me with food."

A deluge of fury engulfed Girija.

'You think I touched somebody who does not observe madi? Are you implying that I should have doused myself with water before I made the puris?' The words were on the tip of her tongue, but she held them back. Girija's patience was inexhaustible. She knew that once she shattered the wall of restraint she had so carefully built around herself there would be

---

[1] small pats of unleavened dough that puff up when deep fried.
[2] a light meal.

no more peace in the house. Once again the wall closed around her confining her.

She took the untouched food back to the kitchen. She heard the children return with Ratna, chattering happily.

"Hi! Mummy! We've brought back hot vegetable samosas[1]...."

Whenever the children brought home snacks from outside, Girija would move away and snap, "Do you have to fall over me? Take it inside."

In this family, none of the elders ever shared the children's simple pleasures or cultivated a meaningful relationship with them.

"Giri, the children have bought you something special. Eat it before it gets cold. You idiots! Where are the plates?"

Charu brought the plates.

Hot samosas. Sweet malai barfi[2].

Ratna mixed the sherbet and added ice cubes. "Rose milk for me, aunty," Bharath clung to her.

Girija joined the happy circle in the drawing room. She enjoyed the T.V. serial and was amused by the noisy comments it evoked from the children. Like the snail which wants to free itself of its shell, she longed to be herself. Thunder roared, the sky turned dark and suddenly lightning flashes of fear as sharp as diamond needles began to stab her.

FOUR ....

The next day Maya's child was still unwell, so Giri had to wash the clothes. While she was on the terrace folding them, she heard Roja Mami's voice.

"How distressing! As if you expect a grand five course feast every day! You are used to a handful of food, prepared according to madi rules. Is that a reason to starve you? It is no hardship looking after you. Mami, you are like a mother to me.

---

[1] savoury patties.
[2] wedges of sweet thickened cream.

I'll make you something, kesari[1], puri or avil kanji[2] with my own hands, and bring it in the evening." Yesterday's incident was being given a new twist. It shocked Giri.

It was a weekday, Ratna was at the University and the children at school.

"It's not Giri's fault, Roja. It's all because of that odious girl. In all these years, Giri has never once let me go to bed hungry. If she has the slightest doubt, she takes a bath before she cooks my evening meal. I don't know what is in store for me now that this creature has come to stay. Kavitha and Charu never come to see me. Look at the way they dress. They are fully grown girls yet they wear only dresses when they go out.

"Last night I went hungry to bed while they gorged themselves on the snacks they had bought. You should have heard their shrieks of laughter. I would never have believed that Girija could behave like this. I wonder how much more I will have to endure!"

"Che!..Che...! You poor thing. I can't bear to see you so unhappy. They say a widow is tortured by her husband's people. But, here we have a daughter-in-law taking advantage of her husband's absence to torture her old mother-in-law. How could she be so heartless to an old woman? Let me ask her for an explanation!"

"Ayyo!..Don't, Roja. Once my son returns, she will become herself again. I'll make him drive that devil out of the house..."

Girija could not remain silent any longer. She walked in.

"Here I am Mami. Did you want to ask me anything?" Roja flashed her a smile and asked, "Hasn't Maya turned up? Why are you folding the clothes yourself?" Even the tone of Roja's voice had changed. Brilliant red kumkumam, an insincere smile, a wrinkled face that was heavily made up, dyed hair, thinly pencilled eyebrows: she looked like an old performing monkey, all dressed up. Girija was furious. "Hasn't Maya come?" Roja asked again.

"Yesterday Amma refused the puris and milk I gave her and now she complains that I starved her. I am sure you believe her."

Giri's pride was hurt and her voice trembled. Unlike Roja, she did not have a gift for innuendo.

---

[1] a sweet dish made of semolina.
[2] porridge made of flattened rice.

"Look Giri, it is best to speak plainly. You may ask me what right I have to interfere. Your father-in-law thought of me as his eldest daughter, long before you entered the family. When my father brought me to Delhi after my marriage, I stayed here, before I set up house on my own. In those days, Ramakrishnapuram was a wilderness. I came in the month of Thai[1] when it was bitterly cold. Your mother-in-law welcomed me with avial[2] and coconut milk payasam. Their flavour still lingers on my tongue. Your parents-in-law lived in spacious quarters in Curzon Road. I used to spend all the nine days of Navarathri[3] here with them. My husband would drop me here and pick me up on his scooter. When he first went to Japan for three months, I stayed again with your parents-in-law. Samu was a difficult child to feed, but he liked chapathis[4] spread with pickle, which I used to make for him."

Roja Mami took pleasure in driving home the point that she had privileges which were denied to Girija.

"Mami observed madi even in those days. Despite the cold, Mama performed his puja very early in the morning in the month of Margazhi[5]. Mami made pongal[6]. A beautiful kolam adorned the courtyard before the sun rose."

"Why stir up all this now, Roja? The past seems like a dream in the face of today's harsh reality. It's nearly twenty years since my husband died."

Roja reminiscenced: "Sarayu was not yet married. Samu had just started his M.A., or had he finished?"

Mamiyar corrected her. "He was doing his course in chartered accountancy in Madras when my husband died. He was not ill but in a matter of seconds, it was all over."

Girija had listened to this story over and over again, but it moved her deeply every time she heard it.

"Since then I have been denied the good fortune to use turmeric and wear kumkumam the symbols of a lady whose

19

---

[1] January—February the harvest season.
[2] a South Indian dish of mixed vegetables delicately spiced.
[3] nine-day Hindu festival marking Goddess Durga's victory over the dark forces.
[4] unleavened bread.
[5] the most auspicious month in the Tamil calender.
[6] savoury rice dish.

husband is alive. What a wretched life!" The old eyes brimmed with tears and she wiped them with a corner of her sari.

"When my husband died, my sons did not allow me to wear a widow's narmadi or shave my head. I did not protest at that time. Later, I realised that as a widow, anyway my presence at my daughter Sarayu's wedding would be considered inauspicious. You know, even if a drop of water from a widow's wet hair falls to the ground, her dead husband is doomed to rouravathi[1] hell for fourteen thousand years. I was distraught. How could I inflict such suffering on my husband? A woman is nothing without her husband. So... I went to Rameshwaram and had my head shaved. Now I can receive theertham[2] from Swamigal, which means that I have to observe the rules of madi more strictly. This is why I have to put Girija to a lot of trouble, although it hurts me to do so. After all she is a young girl...."

Never again, never. All Girija's powers of reasoning, all her rational thoughts deserted her. Her heart melted.

Five

. . . .

"Come in Abu, Come in."
Girija came out of the kitchen, on hearing Ratna's voice. She saw a tall young man with glasses and long hair brushing the nape of his neck. The two furrows on his forehead gave him an air of maturity. He wore a jubba[3] and had a jolna[4] bag slung over his shoulder. "This is Abu, He's working on a project like mine. Abu, meet my aunt Girija." Ratna made the introductions in English.

Abu joined his palms in greeting. With a smile and a nod, Giri invited him into the drawing room.

---

[1] one of the terrible lower worlds in Hindu cosmology.
[2] water used in the worship of an idol and later distributed to the devotees.
[3] a loose collarless shirt, worn by men.
[4] a cloth bag with a long broad strap.

"I've promised him a cup of your excellent coffee, Giri," continued Ratna in English..

Girija smiled.

"Ratna has told me a lot about you," Abu switched to Tamil.

Giri went in to make coffee. Both the girls were out, Charu at her dance class and Kavitha at a friend's place. Bharath was on the terrace flying kites with Malhotra's grandson. Girija had made sojji[1] for Mamiyar. Ratna walked into the kitchen and opened the refrigerator.

"Giri, is there anything to eat?"

"There is thenkozhal in that container."

"Wow! I can smell the cardamom in the sojji!"

Without any hesitation, Ratna served out helpings of sojji and the thenkozhal onto two plates and was about to leave the kitchen, when Giri asked her in a pained voice, "Why didn't you wait for me to serve you?"

Ratna turned towards Giri. Giri went on, "Your patti refused to eat yesterday because she felt that the food was polluted. Do you want to provoke another scene?" Ratna smiled sweetly and carried the plates into the drawing room. She returned for cold water.

"Ratna, you will never understand my predicament. Don't wreck my peace of mind."

"No, I have to do something about this custom. You are a part of this society, you are not an isolated individual. You are not utilising your talents as a teacher. Do you have to sacrifice yourself to this idiotic concept of madi? The observance of madi cannot be justified as it creates barriers between people. Those who observe it are self righteous and arrogant and trample on those who don't. Observance and non observance of it alienates one woman from another."

"You're here only for a couple of days, so it's easy for you to talk so recklessly. Your Chittappa will not let anyone oppose his mother."

"Let him return, I'll talk to him. Come, Abu wants to ask you a few questions. Do you know what his project is about?

21

___
[1] sweet made from semolina.

It is about educated women like you, who, though possessing the power, the shakti,[1] that education endows them with, contribute nothing to society and waste their skills.

Giri felt as though she was teetering on the edge of a precipice.

She served the coffee.

Abu stood up respectfully and took the cup from her.

"Sit down, Giri." Ratna forced her to sit on the sofa. The crystal chandelier glittered in the evening light filtering through the curtains. She was a stranger in her own drawing room with its pleasing blue green patterned wallpaper and the curios visible through the glass doors of the recessed cupboards.

Abu pointed to a batik[2] wall hanging. "Where did you buy this?"

"We didn't buy it. It was a gift from an overseas visitor."

Abu said "I think it is from Bali."

Giri confessed, "I've never looked at it properly."

"Can't you make out that it is a scene from the *Ramayanam*?"

Ratna laughingly said, "Oh, yes. I can spot Hanuman[3]."

"Are you sure it's Hanuman?" Giri took a closer look at the hanging. How stupid of her not to have looked at it closely. She was not sure. Who was it, if not Hanuman...

Abu pointed out, "Can't you make out Sugriva[4], Rama and Lakshmana? You can see the trees in the background. Don't you remember that Rama demonstrated his prowess in archery to Sugriva?"

Giri looked at it closely for the first time.

Rama was on the point of drawing his bow. Could it be the scene where Rama had pierced seven tree trunks with a single arrow?

"The picture has been here for over two years. But I've never looked at it till now." Giri felt ashamed.

"Haven't you ever been curious about it?"

---

[1] the female principle especially personified as Durga, the wife of Shiva; supernatural energy embodied in the female principle.

[2] a process of dyeing and staining cloth originated in Malaysia.

[3] the monkey-god, Lord Rama's greatest devotee.

[4] a monkey whom Lord Rama crowned king of the monkey army.

"Hm.. I studied batik, long ago. But all that seems to belong to another life." She smiled wanly.

"Ratna tells me you taught for eight years. Did you decide not to teach after getting married? Did your husband's people insist that you give up your job?"

"No, Nothing like that".

"Does that mean that it was your own decision?"

Giri felt as nervous as if she was facing a trial.

She had taught for eight years in a village school near Chingleput and had earned the school an excellent name. At the same time she had done her M.A. in English Literature. Had any one appreciated her achievements?

On the contrary, her brother had disapproved strongly. "Why does she want to work in a remote village? If she were in Madras, it would be much easier to find a suitable match for her." Her sister had added, "Who asked her to do her M.A.? Now we'll have to find a boy better qualified than she".

Her mother had fretted, "She is thirty! And should be wearing a thali by now."

Her mother wrote a succession of letters to Girija. "I have taken a vow to offer archanai[1] to Durga during the rahukalam[2] period every Friday in the month of Adi[3]. Please come on a Friday and light a lamp in the temple. Swamigal assured me that you will get married by the month of Thai."

Conditioned by such an environment and nourished on such beliefs, how could Giri think rationally?

The elderly headmaster in her school raised no objection when she wanted to go on leave. She went to the temple on a Friday, cut a lime in half, squeezed out the juice, turned the halves inside out, filled the hollows with ghee and lit wicks in them in the presence of the deity.

She did not ask God for much. Only that her husband should not be unsightly, cruel or a drunkard. The possibility of opening a bank account and depositing her personal savings in it had never occurred to her. Her thoughts had been effectively

23

---

[1] mode of worshipping by chanting the many names of God while offering flowers.

[2] inauspicious hours of the day.

[3] the Tamil month that falls in July—August.

circumscribed by her narrow upbringing, that incarcerated her within the walls of tradition. She could not think for herself.

"The boy is a chartered accountant. He has a post graduate degree in management. His elder brother is married and lives in Canada. His younger sister is also married and has a family. His mother is with him. Financially they are quite sound. The Mamiyar has not asked for jewels or dowry and will be satisfied with a simple marriage ceremony." Giri's mother was very happy.

The day before the wedding, her Mamiyar had sent for her and had presented her with diamond ear studs which weighed one and quarter carats and two nose rings, one of which had nine diamonds and the other four. Girija had had only one side of the nose pierced at that time. Mamiyar had insisted that she should have the other side pierced. Girija's family had been dazzled by the diamonds.

They had never tired of repeating, "Girija is lucky to have such a generous Mamiyar. She is sure to look after Girija well. Which Mamiyar would have parted with her diamonds before the actual ceremony? The ear studs alone must be worth twenty thousand." They had anticipated no problems for Girija. It was also taken for granted that she would give up her job. "He earns five thousand rupees. Why should she even think of working?" Girija and her husband had spent the first few years after their marriage in Bombay and had then moved to Madras, where Bharath was born. And now they were in Delhi where Mamiyar felt at home, since she had lived there for several years.

"You haven't answered me. Was it your personal decision to leave the job?"

"The question never arose. I worked till I got married. There was no economic compulsion to work after marriage. I went to Bombay. I never thought of going back to work."

"All right. Bombay was new to you. But what about the enthusiasm with which you did your M.A and then taught? Do you mean to say that you did not enjoy that?"

"How can you say that? I was full of enthusiasm and always ready to try out innovative methods of teaching at every level. Most of the children in my school belonged to poor families. I achieved excellent results. Let me give you an example. There was a girl whose mother was a thief and father a drunkard. The mother forced the child to steal. The school uniform provided a respectable facade. When she was caught by the police, the headmaster was determined to expel her because she had brought disgrace to the school. I coached the child myself for two years. She finished her tenth standard and left."

Ratna added sarcastically, "Wonderful! And now you have become an insect always lurking in the kitchen." Giri's defences crumbled visibly.

"I seem to have forgotten what I once was. I am not even able to help my own children with their studies. Kavita scored only forty per cent in English and has to be tutored. I am very upset."

"Didn't you think at the time of your wedding that you would be denied all your basic rights?"

"What can I do? It is too late."

Ratna took her hand. "Better late than never".

"What can I do now? Who will run this house if I go out to work?"

Abu said, "It's a great pity that in spite of all your talents, you have become a stranger to your children. You have not even bothered to notice the batik wall hanging in your own house. You have shut your mind to serious social issues. You have isolated yourself from the rest of the world and become submerged in a monotonous existence. Have you thought about the shakti lying locked up and unused within homes like yours? Don't you realise that you too have a role to play to correct the shortcomings and problems of society?"

Abu sipped his coffee slowly. "Ratna was right. The coffee is excellent." He smiled and added, "Forgive me if I have rattled you."

"Oh no, I've had a very dissatisfied feeling deep within me. But nine out of ten people feel that a woman should go out to work only if she needs money. They do not think she has the right to work and that it is important for her intellectual development and for the fulfillment of her individuality. So she gets stuck in a groove."

"All right. Please read the questionnaire I give you carefully and fill it up at leisure. This is not just an exercise. It is meant to motivate you..."

25

3

He handed her a long typed sheet from his bag.

She glanced at the questions.

Name, age, educational achievements, place of birth, caste, details concerning family members — did she belong to a joint family or a nuclear one? What were her views on the family system? Was a dowry given at the time of her marriage? How would she bring up her sons, her daughters? What did she think about fidelity in marriage? How did running a home affect her social life? Was it possible for man and woman to achieve equal status in a real life situation? What role should a woman play in order to establish this equality?.... There were many questions in this vein.

Abu got up to leave. Ratna accompanied him to the end of the street. Girija carefully put away the sheet of paper under a box in the puja cupboard and went in for her bath.

When Ratna returned, Girija was wringing out a wet sari because she had to be in madi clothes to serve her mother-in-law.

"This is unbelievable! After all that Abu said, you've gone back to where you were!"

Giri did not meet her eye. She only said, "Once you break a cage, you cannot stay in it any longer. Don't push me to decide in haste."

Yes, it was not easy for Giri to make up her mind; once she did, there would be no compromise, no going back.

SIX

Girija's husband always returned from his business trips with a pile of dirty clothes and it was her responsibility to get them washed and ironed.

He acknowledged it openly only once. He told Giri that during a ten day seminar abroad, Mrs Menon, his colleague, had complained, "I paid the equivalent of forty rupees to get my sari ironed. How do you manage, Sam?" He had replied,

"Every time I get back, my wife gets all my clothes laundered and stacks them neatly in the wardrobe." What did Samu do when he was away from home for three months? Girija had not asked nor was she told.

She tidied the wardrobe and put away the clean clothes. A beautiful box on the top shelf caught her eye. It was a coral coloured box with exquisite green enamel inlay work.

How had it got there? Had he bought it and forgotten to tell her?

She took out the heavy box, the size of a small briefcase. The key hole was cleverly concealed by an enamel work disc. The box was locked and there was no sign of the key.

She had always trusted him implicitly. There were no secrets between them. What could the box contain?

The box kept intruding on her thoughts all day.

It had definitely not been in Samu's suitcase when she had emptied it. Did it contain anything unusual....

Ratna had moved to a hostel in the morning. She would return later to meet Samu when she would also collect the completed questionnaire. She might bring Abu along. Was Abu a Christian? Abraham? Abubakkar? Abath Sahayam? Whoever he was, he was different.

Girija thought of Kalpana who had made a mess of her life. In comparison hers was serene. But... was she really contented? Be honest, Girija, are you happy? Do you look forward eagerly to each new day? True, Samu had made her his mother's slave. But in all fairness he had no bad habits; he did not drink or smoke, nor was he interested in other women. There had been no secrets between them, at least not till now. He was authoritative by nature. She had always given in to him. Even when she was ill, had he offered to help with the house work? Had he bothered to ask her if she had seen a doctor? She had had to go to the doctor on her own, buy her medicines, and somehow recover and quickly get back to the eternal grind. However, he always brought the house down even if he had the slightest headache.

The ring of the telephone startled her.

"Hello, Giri, I am leaving for Bombay by the evening flight and then going on to Trivandrum. I'll be away for a week, so pack enough clothes. I don't have much time."

Click! Samu had hung up. He rang her only when he needed something done. He came in like a hurricane and left a trail of disorder behind.

Girija had to take care of every detail. Keep both fruit juice and coffee ready for him. Prepare a meal in case he wanted to eat.

Life in this house was a perpetual rush. Life in the outside world must surely be tranquil...

Girija tried to picture Samu relaxing, his tie loosened, in his air conditioned office. He had a pretty secretary with painted lips and manicured nails. Did he find her attractive? Che! Samu was not like that.

But the box?

She had a chance to ask him about it before he left for the airport. While he combed his damp hair in front of the wardrobe mirror after a shower, she asked, "Where did this box come from? What does it contain? Did you forget to mention it?"

Evidently puzzled he asked, "What...?"

She took the box out of the wardrobe.

"Oh you mean this! Roja Mami asked us to keep it for her. She and her husband are probably going to the States to fix up Vivek's marriage."

'How strange! Roja Mami's house in Tagore Avenue is like a fortress with security guards at the gate. Sambasivan, their cook, is very trustworthy. They also have a locker in the bank. Why ask us to keep the box for them? Does it contain something valuable? Jewellery?'

The words trembled on her lips, but as usual, she did not utter them.

She merely asked, "What is in the box? Jewellery?"

He flared up. "Don't pester me with questions. It's getting late. What have you made, rice or chapattis?"

"Do you have to bring the roof down? Is my job only to cook rice and chapathis and never ask questions? You feel your mother is always right. But even a simple question from me makes you fly into a rage," she muttered under her breath and moved away.

The humiliations that she suffered in this house continually pierced her like a many spiked nerunji-thorn[1].

Girija served Samu's rice and left it on the table. She plonked down a bottle of cold water next to it.

"Hey Giri, what is the matter? What were you muttering?"

She did not reply.

He came near and glowered at her. "Why are you sulking?"

She shouted, "I am not sulking. When I open my mouth, you get annoyed. When I am silent, you give me dirty looks. Am I a machine with no feelings at all?"

She burst into angry tears.

He flung his plate to the ground and hurled the bottle to the floor where it shattered.

"Go to hell! This house is as gloomy as a crematorium. I never see a smile on your face when I return from office. You are either muttering to yourself or sweating over the stove. Che! You seem to think of cooking as an unavoidable chore. Look at the dreadful food you serve me. There was too much salt in the lunch you packed today and you forgot the spoon."

"Must you shout senselessly just because I forgot a spoon for once?"

"Who is shouting senselessly? You or I? You think the entire burden of the household is on you and you can do what you please. I won't tolerate disparaging remarks about my mother. If you don't like me or my mother, get out. We can run the house without you. Don't destroy my peace of mind."

He picked up the suitcase which Giri had packed and stalked out.

Che! Didn't people like her husband and Mamiyar have any feelings? Wasn't the burden of the entire household on her shoulders? Hadn't she worked like a slave for seventeen years? Hadn't she borne and brought up three children? Didn't she have the right to ask a simple question? She had not even raised her voice. This cage in which she lived was so constrictive that a mere question became a major transgression: Ratna was right; this was repression at its worst, insidious and severe. What was

---

[1] the thorn of a poisonous plant.

the use of having provided her with creature comforts and gadgets if the woman in her was denied the right to speak?

Even servants would not tolerate such censure. Was it an unpardonable crime to have forgotten a spoon or added too much salt?

In seconds, seventeen years of their marriage had been wiped out. He had flung the plate on the floor, broken the bottle and stormed out. How easy it had been for him!

He had callously dismissed her selfless devotion, trampled on her innermost feelings and crushed the values which she cherished. He was the pivot of her existence, yet he treated her like a worm. Everyone knew that he was hot tempered. She had often been the target of his fury. She knew he was devoid of compassion. She had endured infinite pain. The walls of patience which she had built up so carefully around herself were now in flames.

The doors of the wardrobe were flung open, food had been splattered on the floor. There were splinters of glass everywhere. She had to clean it all up.

"Amma, I can't find my sharpener," complained Bharat.

"Stay right there! Your father broke a bottle and there are pieces of glass all over".

"Amma, the dance master wants the address you promised to get from Appa."

"Don't move! There is broken glass on the floor. Ask the dance master to get in touch with Appa."

She gave the children their morning meal, scrubbed the kitchen and made the beds.

Mamiyar pretended that nothing unusual had occurred. It was just as well that she had been served her meal before the storm broke.

Giri sat on the bed and concentrated on Abu's questionnaire. The new dimensions of her caged existence oppressed her. Sleep eluded her for a long time.

How much longer could she go round and round in this cage? This question germinated in her mind and soon took root.

She went about her morning chores mechanically, but her mind functioned on a totally different plane. She did not speak to Mamiyar or the children. She went through the motions of housework as though she had no connection with it.

She wanted to go to Ratna's hostel and hand over the completed questionnaire. A strong urge to get away from the house for a couple of days took hold of her.

She tried to contact Ratna over the telephone while Maya washed clothes in the bathroom.

There was no response.

She was on her way to the terrace when Mamiyar called out from the doorway of her room "Were you telephoning for cooking gas? The last cylinder has hardly lasted twenty days."

Appappa! Nothing escaped her. She must have known of her son's outburst. Yet she behaved as though nothing had happened.

The diamonds in Girija's ears and nose now seemed like symbols of bondage.

She had not really been aware of being trapped in a cage, until now. Now that she was, the desperate urge to taste freedom for at least a short while made every moment a torture.

31

She removed her diamonds. She put on simple gold earrings, wore her watch on one wrist and a thin bangle on the other. She removed all her chains except the one with her thali.

She packed saris and underclothes in a zipped bag.

Maya had left, Mamiyar had had her morning meal.

She left the bag in the front verandah, bolted the main door and went into Mamiyar's room, as she normally did before going out.

"Why have you taken off your jewels?"

"They need to be cleaned. I am going to the market to buy provisions."

She left the room without waiting for a reply. She picked up the bag and walked briskly down the street.

Mrs Mulay and her children were at the bus stop. They exchanged smiles. Sushma from the house opposite breezed past in a bright yellow salwar kameez. "Auntie, where are you off to with an airbag?"

"To see a friend."

"There is a Spic Mackay programme of South Indian music today. Would you like to come? Shall I give the tickets to Kavita?"

"Who is the artiste?"

"I don't know. It is a violin recital."

"Okay."

A mini bus arrived.

Girija had never elbowed her way determinedly into a Delhi bus before. However, unwilling to linger at the bus stop, she pushed her way in.

The sign on the bus said that it terminated at Delhi railway station.

She bought a ticket and squeezed herself into a space beside an obese Sardarji. The mini bus wheezed to a stop at the bus terminus.

SEVEN

In the scorching heat of the noonday sun, huge, long distance buses coated with dust, lined the sides of the congested terminal.

Raucous voices hawking a mind-boggling variety of things, ranging from bales of cloth to ginger murabba[1] and fine toothed combs assailed the ear.

Apples were in season. A vendor, pushing a cart piled high with the golden variety, called out to Girija to buy his fruit.

She filled her bag with a kilo of apples, bought for five rupees after bargaining with the vendor.

Girija's unapproachable air discouraged any conversation from fellow travellers.

She did not feel guilty nor did she think that she was being deceitful. She had escaped from her cage for a short spell of peace.

She did not consider this in anyway unnatural. She went from bus to bus checking their destinations.

---

[1] ginger soaked in syrup.

Dehra Dun, Rishikesh, Haridwar, Roorkee, Meerut.

The entire family had visited Haridwar, Rishikesh, Benaras and Gaya two years ago on a pilgrimage. Since Mamiyar was with them, Girija had had to cook all the meals. Although it had been a change, she had not been free to do as she pleased.

In her first year as a teacher, the elderly headmaster of her school had organised a trip to North India during the summer vacation. The group of twenty-four consisted of five unmarried girls like Girija as well as middle-aged and elderly couples.

When Girija first told her family about the proposed trip which was to cost only one thousand five hundred rupees, her brother said flatly, "No. It is a waste of money."

Her mother had echoed, "With that money you can buy two or three sovereigns of gold to make jewelry. You'll surely have a chance to travel when you get married. Why do you want to go now?"

Girija had stood her ground. "Why shouldn't I go when all my friends are going? I'm not interested in gold or jewelry." Finally she had cajoled her mother into letting her go.

The memory of that glorious holiday was still fresh in her mind. Uma, Ganga, Parvati, Savitri and Girija had become children again. They had teased the elderly headmaster and his wife. They had sung lustily. They had laughed a great deal. In retrospect the month long holiday seemed a wonderful experience of unalloyed and perfect freedom.

The group had stayed in the Madrasi Dharmsala[1] at Haridwar. The waters of the Ganga had lapped against the steps at the back of the building.

She wished she could sit forever on the balcony and gaze endlessly at the Ganga as it flowed past...

She stood for a minute, lost in old memories and then took hold of herself.

If she were to go back to Haridwar, watch the Ganga flow and free herself from thoughts of the past and present, she might perhaps find peace and a solution to her predicament. She could not decide in haste. From time immemorial the family has been an institution which imperceptibly bound man

33

---

[1] free lodging for pilgrims.

to his kith and kin and it has been woven into the fabric of tradition. But some families had become like monstrous thorn bushes that inflict pain on womankind. Could the concept of family then be wrong?

"Yemma![1] Is this the bus for Haridwar?"

Girija turned around.

An elderly lady and her husband had addressed her. The suitcase and bag they carried looked as worn as they.

"Yemma, you look like a Tamilian. Does this bus go to Haridwar?"

"Yes, it does...let's get in."

She took the suitcase from the old woman and assisted her into the bus. It was obvious that the old man could not see very well. Giri gave him also a helping hand. All three found seats in the same row.

"Yemma, are you also going to Haridwar?"

"Yes, where are you from?", asked Girija.

"We belong to a village near Madurai. For the past five days we have been staying with a relative at Karol Bagh. He wanted to see us off, but could not get leave today. He advised us, 'Take an auto-rickshaw to the bus terminus. There is a bus to Haridwar every half an hour. You won't find it difficult.' But no one is helpful here. You say this bus goes to Haridwar. Why does the name on the bus begin with an 'A'? The 'H' is missing. We cannot read the Hindi script. To our good fortune we found you.... God is great." The old woman rattled on.

The bus gradually filled up: plump Gujarati matrons in white muslin sarees, women from Uttar Pradesh with covered heads and sindoor[2] in the parting of their hair, village men with top knots, children in large numbers.

Girija would never feel alien in this milieu. She was back in the world once familiar to her.

"What time does the bus leave?" asked the old woman.

Girija turned to a man in the next seat and asked in Hindi, "Kitne baje ko bus nikalthi hai?"

He replied, "Ek gante mein. Sade panch, che baje to pahunchthi hai."

---

[1] a term of address used to attract the attention of a strange woman.

[2] vermilion worn in the parting of the hair as a sign of marriage.

Girija explained what he had just said to the old woman, "The bus will leave in an hour and reach Haridwar by five thirty or six o' clock".

"I hope we reach before dark. Our relative has sent a letter of introduction to the Srimadam[1]. We can stay in their choultry[2] which provides food for three days. Where will you stay? You seem to be a working woman."

"I am a teacher. I live in Delhi. I felt like spending two restful days on the banks of the Ganga, so here I am. Though I have friends there, I prefer to stay in a choultry. It doesn't worry me, Mami."

The driver and conductor boarded the bus.

The bus made its way through the crowded roads of the city and crossed the Yamuna which was flowing majestically.

"Mother Yamuna! Krishna! Krishna! Whenever I look at a river I am filled with ecstasy. I sat up all night on the train to Delhi just to see the Krishna and Godavari. I missed the Narmada. We saved all our life to afford this journey. Now, we are at the very end of our lives. We have had a good trip so far. We don't mind if we cannot go to Badrinath, but we must have a dip in the Ganga at Haridwar and Rishikesh. We were warned to hold on to the chains because the current is strong. I hear that the Swamigal is in Haridwar." The old woman's incessant chatter soothed Girija.

The bus halted at Meerut. The old woman took out a flask from her bag and poured a cup of coffee for her husband. His hands trembled, so she had to guide the cup to his lips. She offered Girija a cup of coffee.

"Have a mouthful," she urged.

"No, no, Mami, I have fruit with me."

"So what! There's plenty of coffee. I can't finish all of it. Let us share it. The milk in Delhi is excellent."

She could not refuse, so she drank the coffee. No one had ever offered her coffee with such concern.

This simple act of kindness gave a special flavour to the coffee.

---

[1] the spiritual centre/seat of a religious leader/teacher.
[2] lodging for pilgrims.

By the time the bus reached Haridwar, the old woman developed a fondness for Girija and launched into the story of her life. Her husband was descended from a long line of village munsiffs[1]. They had had six children, but none had survived. Their three sons had died in infancy, and two of the girls at birth. A third daughter had succumbed to diarrhoea when she was barely twenty days old.

It was obvious from the old woman's tale that the munsiff husband had had all the qualities that went with his position — haughtiness, the arrogance of belonging to a higher caste, and an autocratic manner. Her cruel mother-in-law had lived to be ninety. Her husband's arrogance and caste-consciousness had brought them untold misery and had eventually cost him his position. He had lost all his money, sold his old house, the barren land and his meagre possessions to his nephew. This money was spent to make the yatra[2] to the sacred Ganga which had been their life-long desire.

"Don't be misled by his docile appearance," said the old woman," I'll say to his face that he used to beat me with firewood at his mother's instigation. He insulted the tahsildar[3] by calling him a low-class scoundrel. The tahsildar retaliated by suspending him on trumped up charges. One problem after another..."

The bald, shrivelled, half blind old man wearing a dis-coloured checked shirt and tattered woollens, was huddled in a corner, totally dependent on his wife for companionship and support. Would Samu be like him when he grew old? No, they belonged to different eras. The old man belonged to the era of caste arrogance and petty tyrannies, and Samu to the era

---

[1] rural officer of the law.
[2] any journey, in this case a pilgrimage.
[3] revenue official in charge of a subdivision of a district.

of money, power and ostentatious living. He would not need her in his old age.

The old woman was as fiercely protective of the man as a bird with its young. She talked about the way he had treated her without the slightest trace of bitterness. Girija wondered how the old woman would react to Abu's questionnaire.

The old woman had been conditioned to believe that the purusha[1], the husband, was both the sthula[2] and sukshama sarira[3], the perceived and unperceived form of God, who gave refuge to his wife who was like a wisp of straw in the waves of the ocean. The man had the right to beat his wife, to crush her, and tyrannise her. It was her duty to serve, worship and cherish him.Only the husband had a right to own property. When a woman married, she became part of her husband's family. If she deserted him, his people would disown her. She could have nothing more to do with her son. A daughter, anyway did not belong to her parents; she was born only to become a slave to her husband's family.

The bus reached Haridwar at nightfall. Fortunately for the old couple, Girija spoke Hindi. She engaged a rickshaw for them.

"You're here only for two days. Why don't you stay with us? We can see Haridwar together." Here was the invitation that Girija had been hoping for. She got into another rickshaw and all of them set out for the choultry. The choultry was the same one in which she had stayed as a young girl. However, it had changed hands. The Ganga still lapped at the steps at the back of the building.

It was time for evening deeparati[4]. Gowri Ammal, the old woman, made her husband sit on the steps and poured the water of the holy Ganga over him with a copper vessel. Girija joined them and sat on the wide steps leading to the water. The invigorating touch of the icy water drained her of all her pent up emotions.. She lost herself in the flow of the Ganga; the past and the present seemed to dissolve...

---

[1] the male energy.
[2] the perishable body.
[3] the imperishable inner being.
[4] worship performed with lamps.

NINE

I n the morning, Girija rose early, brushed her teeth and carrying a change of
clothes, proceeded towards Hari-ki-Pairi, the wide steps leading
to the Ganga. Shops displaying a medley of wares lined the
narrow streets leading to the bathing ghats. Women on their
way to the ghat gazed longingly at the glittering jewels and
saris. Vessels and travel trunks were seen side by side with bell-
metal idols for worship and containers of brass, aluminium and
plastic for collecting the holy water of the Ganga. Milk was
already on the boil in huge cauldrons over newly lit stoves
at the sweet vendors'. At the tea stall, fresh milk was being
delivered for morning tea. People jostled each other in the
streets. Even though they were from distant corners of India,
their regional identities were easy to establish. Householders,
ascetics, youngsters, old people, those who had just arrived by
train carrying bags, those who had made the banks of the Ganga
their permanent home, all milled around. The strands of Indian
culture were being woven in the loom of time.

Tiny marble shrines dotted the Hari-ki-Pairi. The steps
teemed with people wringing their clothes dry, as well as
mendicants, givers of alms and greedy pandas[1].

The sea of unfamiliar faces gladdened Giri's heart. An old
Bengali woman, who was drying herself after a dip in the
Ganga, readily promised to keep an eye on her clothes.

Even where it had been dammed, the force of the waters
was awesome. Bathers had to hold on to chains for fear of being
carried away by the current. The force of the mighty Ganga
had swept away the chains and supports beyond the Hari-ki-
Pairi. Girija hitched up her sari and dipped a timid toe into the
water. She could feel the pull of the current.

As a precaution against being swept away by the strong current, pilgrims in twos and threes held hands while bathing. A

---

[1] priests who perform rites.

Gujarati girl with a big dot of kumkumam on her forehead was helping an old woman bathe. With excited cries of "Aoji, Aoji,"[1] she kept the chain of human hands unbroken with infectious enthusiasm. A young man, her husband or brother, sat on the steps enjoying the scene.

The Gujarati girl seeing Girija hesitate, exhorted, "Aoji, Aoji," and extended her hand to draw Giri into the circle. The chain of hands inspired confidence.

Immerse yourself..dip...! What a wonderful feeling! Was this the ultimate bliss? The flow of the Ganga purged one of all sorrows and troubles and gave one clarity of vision.

Dip...dip...! The girl who initiated this chain of hands, though herself afraid to immerse completely, drew more and more people into the circle. Young and old alike, she drove away their fears by reaching out to form new links in the chain. Here was a confluence which transcended the barrier of language, caste and region.

The linked hands infused a sense of security for those few moments. This swift flow of water, this regenerative bath, this was reality. The petty differences of caste, education and language disappeared. The pilgrims returned to firm ground, still holding hands, while newcomers went in.

"Here she is! Yemma, why did you leave without a word?" Girija turned around. Gowri Ammal was guiding her husband by the hand.

"I assumed that you would need time to get Mama[2] ready. Did you have any difficulty in finding your way?"

"Aiyo! The current is strong even here," observed Gowri Ammal. A Punjabi woman infected by the Gujarati girl's exuberance held out her hand and invited them to join.

"Didiji, join us. It is truly exhilarating to bathe here and it is also quite safe. You must bathe in the Ganga after making the long journey to Haridwar. Come, dadaji[3], hold on to didi."

A young couple, Girija and the old pair formed a circle. The translucent water lapped around them and they rejoiced in the experience.

---

[1] "Come and join us."
[2] a friendly and respectful term of address to an older man not necessarily related to one.
[3] paternal grandfather, here a term of respect.

As she plunged in again and again, Gowri Ammal called upon the seven holy rivers to mingle:

"Gangena Yamunaicheva Godavari Saraswathi Narmada Sindu Kaveri jalesmin Sannidhim kuru."[1]

A new Girija, cleansed of her repressed feelings of anger and resentment emerged from the water.

Three days went by swiftly, as she bathed and wandered along the river. Childlike, she revelled in the sweet taste of freedom.

TEN

On the evening of her fourth day at Haridwar, Girija sat on the steps near the bridge and dabbled her feet in the water. It was the hour of the evening deeparati. Ascetics in saffron robes, beautiful young girls and senescent women were making offerings to the swiftly flowing Ganga. Flower vendors made lamps by fashioning tiny boats from leaves each containing a wick dipped in oil and surrounded by flowers. Every devotee bought these lamps and lit the wicks before setting them afloat. A few of these frail crafts with wicks still aglow survived the rapid currents and dangerous whirlpools which were strong enough to destroy even iron chains. When these lamps victoriously floated past the bridge, there was great rejoicing.

Girija reflected on the frenetic lifestyle of the younger generation... Kavi and Charu constantly lived with ear blasting pop music. Their father had bought each of them a walkman which they listened to even while studying. Silence made them restless and bored. How could they enjoy that cacophony? Girija wondered whether her children would overcome the obstacles in the stream of life and emerge unbeaten like these floating lamps....

---

[1] a popular chant before bathing, invoking the sacred rivers of India, "May the rivers Ganga, Yamuna, Godavari, Saraswathi, Narmada, Sindhu and Kaveri be present in these waters."

"Teacher...? Aren't you Girija Teacher?"

Startled, Girija turned around. The voice belonged to a dark-skinned, veshti–clad[1] young man, whose poonal[2] hung loosely across his painfully thin frame. His head had been tonsured in the manner of a South Indian brahmin with a tuft of hair on the crown.

"Who are you? Your face is familiar, though I can't place you," said Girija.

"Don't you recognize me? Aren't you Girija Teacher?"

"Yes?"

"Teacher, I'm Dharmarajan. You used to call me Dharmam. I am Savitri Mami's son. Don't you remember?"

"Oh!"

Yes! She remembered. Savitri had had eight children in quick succession. Saraswathi, the Goddess of learning had not blessed her husband, though he belonged to a family of learned puro-hits[3]. His constant preoccupation with food had made him ill. Savitri was left to support him and their eight children. She had ground batter, rolled out appalams[4], pounded cereal and eked out a living. On auspicious occasions she had helped Girija, who had taken on the responsibility of educating Dharmam and his sister Vimala.

"Amma is no more, teacher. Appa also passed away many years ago. Nanu, my married brother, lives in Bangalore. Vimala teaches in a convent. Sivakami, Chandru and Raju continue to stay in the village. I have come away with Swamigal."

"What do you do for a living?"

"I run errands and do what I am told in the mutt[5], in return for which they give me food. Have you come from Delhi, teacher?"

"Yes."

"Have you had darshan of Swamigal? Did he speak to you?"

She looked down at the water. How could she explain that for her there was no truth beyond the Ganga.

41

---

[1] a length of white cloth worn by men very like a sarong.
[2] the sacred thread.
[3] priests.
[4] savoury crisps.
[5] the establishment of religious or spiritual leader.

"If you like, I can take you to Swamigal and arrange for a good darshan."

His face glowed expectantly. Here was his chance to show her that even he could do something for her.

"That will be nice. I'll let you know."

He pointed to a building. "You can find me in the front room of that building. Come in time for the puja, Teacher."

What strange turns life takes!

Who would have thought Dharmam had it in him to do what he believed was a favour to her. Now, there was no question of letting him down. She would attend the puja.

That night Gowri Ammal and her husband returned late. "Yemma, I looked for you all over. Where have you been? We went to Rishikesh. The sight of the Ganga was truly glorious. We crossed the river to the other bank. Going to all the temples has made our visit memorable. There's just one last wish..."

"What is it, Mami? How can you leave the Ganga with an unfulfilled wish?"

"How we wish we could have darshan of Swamigal and get his blessings! When Swamigal visited our village and performed puja, my father-in-law was the munsiff and it was my husband who made all the arrangements. I'm sure Swamigal will remember my father-in-law."

"Is that all Mami? One of my old students recognised me today. He is working in the mutt and has offered to take me to the Swamigal."

Early next morning, Girija and the old couple set out after a bath and a cup of coffee. They carried a tray laden with kalkandu[1] and fruit as offerings to Swamigal.

They entered the building which Dharmam had indicated. In the front room which served as the office, a man was seated at a low desk. He peered at Girija through his spectacles.

"Where can I find Dharmarajan?" enquired Girija.

"Dharmarajan? Who is he? There is no one of that name here. Where are you from?"

[1] rock candy from sugarcane.

"I...I have come from Delhi." Before Girija could stammer out an explanation, Dharmam walked in. "Ade Ade![1] Come in teacher. I'll take you to meet Swamigal."

"You mean you are looking for this fellow." The man turned to Dharmam and asked derisively, "Hey! Is your name Dharmarajan? We call him asattu pitchu, the nitwit. The name Dharmarajan, Lord of Wisdom, is totally unsuitable for him."

Dharmam introduced Girija to the manager. "She was one of my senior teachers and now lives in Delhi."

"All right. Take them in."

Girija, Gowri Ammal and her husband, all suitably attired for the solemn occasion, followed Dharmam. He entered the room where Swamigal was seated while Girija and her friends stood in the doorway.

Two men stood on either side of Swamigal respectfully covering their mouths with their hands. A stack of files awaited his perusal. Another, sitting deferentially at the feet of Swamigal awaited his instructions to reply to letters. Gowri Ammal's husband recited Sanskrit slokas[2] in a loud voice. Dharmam stood in front of Swamigal in a reverential attitude with joined palms. Time passed. Swamigal gave no indication that he was aware of their presence. Girija whispered in Dharmam's ear, "If he has no time now, we can come back later." Dharmam assured her in sign language that the wait would not be long. At that moment a man came bearing a sack of rice which he placed before Swamigal as an offering. Trays of fruit, like apples, guavas, pomegranates and bananas, varieties of vegetables such as pumpkin, ash gourd, ladies fingers, quantities of pulses, kalkandu, almonds and raisins filled the small room... soon followed by the unmistakable fragrance of Chanel... It was Roja Mami with her husband!

Girija, petrified, flattened herself against the wall. All of a sudden, a smile lit up Swamigal's face. Roja Mami and her husband prostrated themselves at his feet. Roja Mami's dyed hair was wet and loosely knotted with flowers. Diamonds sparkled in her ears and she wore a nine yard sari in the orthodox brahmin manner. She stood respectfully.

43

[1] exclamation meaning Hallo! Hallo!
[2] verses.

She addressed Swamigal unctuously. "By Swamigal's grace, insurmountable obstacles have dispersed like the mist." Her voice was choked with emotion.

"I hope all is well!" said Swamigal. Roja Mami continued, "We have fixed an alliance for our son. The girl and her father Ramakrishnan live in the States. We have come to offer bikshai[1] and to seek Swamigal's blessings."

Both of them again fell at the feet of Swamigal, who gave them kumkumam and akshadai[2] prasadam and blessed them.

Girija moved away from the tight knot of people. Gowri Ammal also received akshadai prasadam. The offerings were quickly whisked away.

"Make way." One of the entourage cleared the way for Swamigal who was on his way to do puja.

Girija slipped out. She overheard the bespectacled manager telling someone, "He retired as Secretary for Steel and is now heading some other prestigious organisation. Both husband and wife are devotees of Swamigal, and known for their hospitality. No visitor to Delhi comes away without having a meal in their house. They are very generous. Men in his position rarely possess such an admirable temperament. He received the Shiromani[3] award from the President for his invaluable services to the country." He continued in a conspiratorial tone, "His detractors, jealous of his reputation, tipped the Central Bureau of Investigation advising them to conduct a raid. Top ranking officials are often targets of such raids." He paused. "They make frequent trips from Delhi for a darshan of Swamigal."

Girija was rooted to the spot. A C.B.I. raid...things fell into place. What did the red enamel box contain? Why was it concealed in their wardrobe? Samu must be in the know. The box must contain valuables worth lakhs, perhaps even crores of rupees. Thoughts criss-crossed in her brain.

Suddenly she panicked. Had Roja Mami seen her? Would she publicly accuse her and take her back by force? Girija made a hasty exit. It would be wiser to give the slip to Gowri Ammal

---

[1] alms received by monks from devotees.
[2] unbroken rice used to invoke God's blessing.
[3] an award for excellence in various spheres of activity.

and her husband. Gowri Ammal who was conservative would surely disapprove of her running away from home. Girija would forfeit her trust and respect. Her neck was bare, except for the gold chain with the thali. They had not asked her whether she was married. Gowri Ammal was tactful. The elderly couple minded their business. Most probably they would be gone by tomorrow.

But what was Girija to do now?

Eleven

An uncontrollable urge, an inexplicable desire, had impelled Girija to leave home. She had torn herself away from her family with the implicit faith that she would find peace on the banks of the Ganga. Even as she was savouring her freedom, the question of what the future held for her tortured her. She was shaken by the fear that Roja Mami would blemish her hitherto unsullied reputation by telling one and all that Girija had run away from home.

It was ironical that the ostentatious circle which she abhorred had followed her like a shadow even to Haridwar.

A tumultuous crowd thronged the Hari-ki-pairi. An old Bengali woman in white muslin held a stack of chapathis and a wide mouthed brass vessel containing yellow dhal[1], which she doled out to beggars. Each beggar received four chapathis and two ladlefuls of dhal. Even the bank of this holy river teemed with wastrels in filthy clothes parading as beggars! Did they fear that they would not receive alms if they were clean?

Girija was filled with revulsion. People thought they were earning salvation merely by distributing food. They sullied the sanctity of the Ganga by their cheap behaviour. She tried to visualize the Ganga in days gone by, when its pristine beauty was not marred by the presence of such crowds.

A cry of "Rishikesh Rishikesh" announced the imminent departure of a nearby bus. She decided to spend the day at Rishikesh and clambered aboard.

---

[1] lentil, cooked and mashed.

Unending vistas of green stretched out on either side of the road. The Ganga disappeared from view. The lushness she bestowed gladdened the eyes. Rivulets frothed along the road-sides. Scenes flashed by: grass cutters, simple women coolies[1] and clusters of children with wistful faces who perhaps wondered why nature's bounty did not ameliorate their lot in life. Did not hoardings displaying the red triangle, the symbol of family planning; accuse the children of being the cause of the nation's poverty?

She was filled with a strong desire to gather them in her arms, to stay with them, to care for them, to be once again a teacher in a small school in this beautiful spot and lead an untrammeled existence.

She allowed her mind to dwell on this pleasant daydream. The river came into view and disappeared as she travelled on the rattling bus which finally ground to a halt in the terminus. The scorching heat of the sun was unbearable.

Girija was jolted out of her reverie. Modernisation had changed the face of Rishikesh. Multi-storeyed buildings had sprung up which hid the Ganga from view. Smelly drains, the deafening noise of traffic and hordes of people assailed her senses.

Where were the beautiful serene ashrams that had dotted the river banks twenty-five years ago? Now a broad road wound its way through the town. Luxurious hotels with air-conditioned rooms, comfortable beds and tasty food beckoned the traveller.

Mother Ganga, where have you gone? Could this place provide an answer to her predicament? The relentless heat enervated her. Having skipped breakfast she was ravenously hungry. But she could not find a restaurant to suit her taste. There were shops selling clothes, vessels and electronic goods. Luckily she found a fruit shop where she bought four apples.

"Gangaji ka kinara kahan hai?" — Where are the banks of the Ganga?

"Seedha jayiye." — Go straight ahead.

She set off briskly her thoughts keeping pace with her steps.

---

[1] labourers who carry loads.

Where were the banks of the Ganga? How would her uncertainties be resolved? Should she return home or not? A decision had to be taken that day on the banks of the Ganga. She felt suffocated by the crowds which destroyed the peace of Rishikesh. The other tourists had not come in search of peace. All they wanted was a whirlwind tour of pilgrim centres—Gangotri, Yamunotri and Rishikesh all in one day—something to boast about on their return home.

Twenty-five years ago, a group of teachers including Girija had visited Haridwar and Rishikesh... Her friend Ganga, the music teacher, was a powerful swimmer, having grown up on the banks of the Thamarabarani[1] river in the extreme south of India. But the older teachers in the group had not permitted her to swim in the Ganga at Haridwar.

"I'll show you how well I can swim," she had challenged her peers. Parvatamma, the Headmaster's wife had scolded her, "This is not a trickle of water like your Thamarabarani. Behave yourself, we have to reach home safely." The whole group had alighted from the bus at Rishikesh and had walked across Lakshman Jhoola, the suspension bridge over the Ganga. The other bank had been a haven of peace.

They had ordered a meal at the choultry run by a pandit and had gone to the river for a dip. Ganga had hitched up her sari and had dived into the blue depths of the river.

Panic stricken cries of "Ayyo! Ayyo![2] Ganga come back!" had rent the air and the teachers had been aghast. Such a foolhardy girl! She had been the boldest of the lot.

Even after twenty-five years, Girija remembered the incident with awe. Ganga had swum back to the bank, her happy face like a lotus in full bloom. She had been like a lighted wick in a leaf boat.

"We concede that you are very daring. Spare us further agony, if you please," old Bhagirathi, the teacher had pleaded. Later...

There was a lump in Girija's throat. Ganga had left school to get married. They had met five years later at a handloom

---

[1] a river of South India.
[2] an exclamation equivalent to "Hello!"

exhibition in Madras. Ganga had introduced her husband and three daughters to Girija. "I have only daughters," she had said with a rueful smile. Girija had replied, "You're a daring swimmer, Ganga. What does it matter if you have only daughters?"

"It is easy to swim in water..." she had stopped in midsentence. Again that rueful pathetic smile. "Are you still single?" Girija was unmarried at that time. "Good for you," said Ganga. Six months later, Girija heard the terrible news.

"Giri, do you remember our Ganga? She's dead. The poor wretch was pregnant for the fourth time. A quack prescribed some medicine which resulted in her haemorraging to death."

What a way to go! Even the river Ganga seemed to weep. Had her husband ordered her to produce a son? Why had she wanted to destroy her unborn child? Had she been afraid that her fourth would also be a girl?

Ganga's beautiful face as she swam ashore was still vivid in Girija's memory. Even if she had been swept away by the current that day, she would still be remembered as a brightly burning wick in a leaf boat. Unfortunately the currents and whirlpools of life had wiped out her courageous spirit and left her vulnerable and afraid of life. Not only was the wick doused by the flowing Ganga, but the boat too had also capsized and sunk without trace. Ganga had been annihilated.

One of Abu's questions seemed to acquire a new significance when applied to Ganga's life. "After marriage would you like to move away from the mainstream of life and live a caged existence where you might lose your identity?" It is true that every woman finds fulfillment in marriage and children. But the very same marriage often strips a woman of her shakti, her life force. Isn't a man responsible for the sex of his child? Yet, only the woman is blamed if she bears a daughter. What would have happened if Girija's third child had also been a girl? This had preyed on her mind when she was expecting Bharath. The mores of society were always inimical to women.

The ground was slushy beneath her feet. The path beside the river bank undulated and became progressively narrow. A truck loaded with building materials roared past. Girija was hemmed in by the crowd. She left the path and climbed up a steep slope. A derelict ashram came into view. Wide arches and the faded words "Om,"[1] "Aushadalaya,"[2] and "Goshala"[3] traced on yellowing walls indicated that the ashram had been a place of importance at one time. From this point she had a clear view of the opposite bank of the Ganga.

Girija sat on an old cement bench and bit into a juicy apple.

TWELVE

"Yemma, Are you a Tamilian?" She turned around on hearing a voice which seemed to emanate from behind the bench on which she was resting.

She saw a tall elderly woman standing upright, with unruly hair like puffs of cotton and a face furrowed by the passage of time. She wore a saffron[4] coloured sari with a blouse of the same colour.

She repeated her question. "Are you a Tamilian?"

"Yes...Patti...!"

"Which is your native place?"

"Madurai, but I have been living in Delhi."

"Have you come alone?"

"I came with friends, who visited Rishikesh yesterday. Today they are attending a special puja at Haridwar, so I am on my own. Are you also a pilgrim Patti?"

The old woman gave a toothless smile.

"It must be about fifty years since I came. The passage of time does not mean much to me any more. The Ganga flows and life goes on...."

"Oh!" Girija was amazed. "What brought you here all those years ago?"

49

---

[1] the primal sound; sacred to Hindus.
[2] a pharmacy for Ayurvedic medicine.
[3] shelter for cows.
[4] a colour associated with renunciation, sacrifice and spartan religious life.

"It just happened. When I came, a Swamiji was occupying this ashram. Now, it is run by a Hindu mission. It has grown and there are rooms for pilgrims to stay."

"Where did you come from?" asked Girija.

"At one stage of my life, from Madurai. Now, this is my home. This is where I belong."

Girija was impressed. Fifty years ago, the old woman could not have been older than she was now. At such a young age, what force or event had prompted her to move away from the mainstream of life, don an ascetic's saffron robes and take refuge in this ashram? Surely, in those days, a girl of her age would have been married? Had she been widowed?

"Yemma, you look tired. Have you had anything to eat?"

Girija smiled. "Some fruit."

"Just fruit? Nothing else?"

"I didn't like the the hotels I saw."

"Don't bother about hotels. Come in and have a handful of rice with buttermilk."

Girija could not quite comprehend what was happening.

On the way from Delhi, Gowri Ammal had spontaneously befriended her and offered her coffee. Now, here in Rishikesh, another total stranger had impulsively invited her for a meal.

"Never eat food offered by strangers. Never touch unattended parcels or suitcases." Girija had been conditioned by these words of warning. At this moment, when she was contemplating breaking away from her orderly existence, these words meant nothing. The course of her life would change.

"Yemma? Are you afraid because you don't know me? Don't worry, it's just a simple meal."

"Have you had lunch?" asked Girija.

"Yes... Come in..."

Girija washed her hands and feet with the chembu of water that the old lady gave her. She entered the hut. An austere rectangular room; an old fashioned mud stove in one corner. The old woman served rice in an aluminium plate and poured thick buttermilk from an earthernware jar over it. Salt and lime pickle lent a piquant flavour to the meal.

To Girija this meal tasted much better than those cooked and served by her mother and mother-in-law at the time she had had her babies.

"I have never tasted such delicious food, Patti, in all the forty-six years of my life. This is an encounter which I'll always cherish."

"On certain days, I feel like cooking an extra portion. Today was one such day. I spotted you climbing the steps from where I was seated. I was happy."

"Patti, I hope you don't mind if I confide in you. I completed my studies and taught in a school for eight years. Then I got married. That was seventeen years ago. I am now in Delhi. To all appearances, I lack nothing. But gone is the sense of fulfillment that I had as a village school teacher. I feel so much at ease with you, maybe because you invited me so spontaneously. What made you seek refuge here? How did you reach these shores? A man can afford to turn his back on his family without any qualms. He doesn't feel that family ties are sacrosanct. A wife and children exist for his convenience. He can discard them if he feels like it. Can a woman have the same attitude? Answer me, Patti?"

"You're quite right. But circumstances can wash one up on strange shores. I used to watch with childish pleasure the deeparati on the Ganga. Some of the lamps used to stray away from the mainstream and run aground on the shore. I felt I was like them. I was born in a poor family in Nagapattinam. There were eight of us. I was the fifth daughter. I was married to a middle-aged widower as his third wife. I had no say in the matter. I was naive. Later, I discovered that my husband's two sons by his previous marriage were already married. It was a large household. In my parents' house, I used to go hungry, but I enjoyed a certain amount of freedom. I used to bathe in the river, visit the temple and help my mother in the house. In my husband's house, my stepson ordered me around. There was nothing specific to complain about. But his behaviour began to make me uneasy. I never felt married, for I saw my husband only at meal times. He was always in a stupor. A month or two went by... A Swamiji came to our town and conducted bhajans[1]. He never stayed for more than three days in any one place. My husband was drawn to the Swamiji and invited him

---

[1] group singing and chanting of sacred verses.

for bikshai. I believe, Swamiji invited my husband to come and stay here for a few days. At that time, this ashram was being built here. I came with him. There was no road to the Ashram then. We left our luggage in a choultry at Haridwar and went to bathe in the Ganga. We were advised to hold on to each other while bathing, because it was the month just before Deepavali[1], and the current of the swiftly flowing Ganga, which was in spate, was strong.

"The current pulled my husband and I .....

"Being sturdy, I was able to pull myself ashore. Helping hands dragged me onto the sand. Normally, no one tries to save a person drowning in the Ganga. "Ganga matha le jathi," Mother Ganga takes away. Death by drowning in the Ganga is considered to be the road to salvation. I was saved. His life was snuffed out."

It seemed as if the world had come to a standstill and that only two beings, the old woman and Giriji, existed.

The old woman did not speak for a while. Girija was reluctant to break the silence.

Patti resumed "Did you notice 'Om Aushadalaya' written on the sign board?"

"Yes..?"

"After I lost my husband, a Swamiji known as Bhavananda admitted me into the ashram. He was a freedom fighter who found himself stranded here. He was then around twenty or twenty-two. He was responsible for dragging me ashore to safety. He was the one who tried to resuscitate my husband with poultices and burning herbs. His efforts proved futile. According to custom, the cremation took place immediately afterwards on the shores of the Ganga. The family could not be informed until later. My stepson came to take me back. How he insulted the brahmachari[2]... Siva...Siva![3]...they were words which cannot be uttered. I hid myself and crossed the jungle to reach the ashram, where I poured out my woes to the senior Swamiji."

"You need not go back. You can stay here," he said.

---

[1] the festival of lights celebrated all over India (October-November).
[2] a celibate.
[3] an exclamation equivalent to "Oh God!"

"So I stayed behind and have been here ever since." Girija doubted whether it had been as simple as the old woman made it out to be.

"Is there no one in the ashram now?.. You seem to be a woman of great courage. I am sure you won't take it amiss, Patti, but it could not have been an easy matter for a woman as young as you to live with young celibates and ascetics. Swamiji must have had his detractors?"

The old woman laughed.

"Flood waters uproot even big trees. That evil stepson wanted to take me back, shave my head, make me wear widow's garb and confine me to a corner of the house. He wanted to take revenge because I had not yielded to him. Back home, he must have torn my reputation to shreds. I was fortunately out of ear shot. The first time I met the senior Swamiji, he was seated on the same cement bench where I found you. He objected strongly to widows being shorn of their hair and ornaments and openly said that it was a sin to do so. He averred that these customs were barbaric and that they were later additions not found in the original code of conduct specified in the Shastras[1]. I was the first woman to join the ashram as an ascetic. Others followed. The brahmachari I referred to was an authority on Ayurveda.[2] He made medicines from herbs. I used to accompany him on his visits to the surrounding villages. Experience is a good teacher. Attending to cases of fever, scabies, pustules, eye sores, earaches and assisting in child birth, I felt I had fulfilled my purpose in life. On bitterly cold nights we used to warm ourselves around a fire. The Swamiji was known as Bishak Baba and I was addressed as Mataji. Rich and poor alike came to the ashram. Unlike today's tourists who come on day trips by cars and buses, those who came stayed on to enjoy the peace..."

"Where is Bishak Baba?"

"He passed away eight years ago. The number of people coming for herbal medicines dwindled. Since I was well trained by him, I used to treat those who continued to come even after

[1] code of social sacraments.
[2] the traditional Indian system of medicine.

Swamiji's death. Now there are more and more doctors who practise western medicine."

"Did you ever go back to South India?"

"I did. We went by foot on a pilgrimage to Kanyakumari, at the southernmost tip of India. But I find peace only in this spot. Times have changed. Do you see that tall building and prayer hall? The mission which now bears the Swamiji's name has expanded. They have built a hospital in town. The rich and powerful come on fleeting visits and stay in the cottages on the other bank of the Ganga. The ideals we cherished have nothing in common with the values of this generation."

Girija listened attentively. Why not confide in this old woman?

"Patti, you are far wiser than those of us who are educated and hold degrees. You are tolerant of even those who come and disturb your peace. What do you feel about modern households and current life styles?"

"The basic outlook of people has undergone a dramatic change. Money is all that matters. I see women who have a dual role to play as housewives as well as bread winners. There are also others like painted dolls, looking unhappy in their chauffeur driven cars. Perhaps they are harassed by their in-laws for not having brought adequate dowries. Some of them are sent back to their parents, because they cannot comply with demands for money from their in-laws. Some of them take the easy way out by jumping into the Ganga."

"Patti, to be frank, I have come to find solace. I have to solve my problems. I have two daughters and a son. I am well off. But, circumstances have reduced me to a machine working unceasingly from morning till night. More over, I am sandwiched between two generations. On the one hand, my children are raring to break out of the cage of convention and on the other, my mother-in-law tortures me with her harsh madi rules. I am a bonded slave to both. I now realise that I am living in a void empty of even an ounce of human feeling. I feel I must get away from it. All those years I spent studying and teaching enriched my life. In the framework of marriage, is the woman's role only one of subservience? How can I continue like this? You yourself admit that you have learnt a lot from experience. Do madi rules really have any relevance in today's context? Why should I continue to bear the burden of outworn traditions? Do you know of any one else in the same predicament?"

Clouds covered the sky and brought relief from the severity of the sun.

The old woman had been listening attentively with half closed eyes.

"I don't know your name, but let me tell you something. As long as you brood on your problems you will remain confused. Follow the advice Swamiji gave me. If the situation becomes unbearable, fight it. After clearly debating the issue, choose the option best suited to you. Once you have decided, don't vacillate. Some contemplate suicide, but it is cowardice and only proves that they lack the courage to solve their problems. I was uneducated and inexperienced when my husband died. After the tragedy, my brother-in-law came to Haridwar and advised me, 'You are very young. If you stay here, it'll cause a scandal. So come back.. The brahmachari is an evil genius!' Admittedly, I did not know what sort of a man the brahmachari was. But I had made up my mind not to go back, come what may. I did not want to face the abject poverty in my parents' house, the cruelty in my husband's home and above all the inevitable barbed insinuations that I was responsible for my husband's drowning. I was unshaken in my decision. I did not want to go back and then regret my action..."

The sky became overcast. The cries of the crowds along the shores of the Ganga quietened. Did the old woman perhaps think that Girija was contemplating suicide? Girija felt embarassed.

"The dark skies forecast heavy rain. Would you like to spend the night here?"

"No, Patti. I have to go back. I had to escape from my mechanical life and come in search of peace. I wanted to think clearly. I'll never forget you. You have not only given me food but to quote Bharathiyar,[1] you have also nourished my intellect and strengthened my body. I have to leave."

---

[1] a well-known twentieth century Tamil poet.

"Take care... Believe me, nothing is impossible. You can shape your own destiny."

At last, Girija was very clear in her mind.

"Your problems are yours to solve. Confront your Mamiyar, who is, after all, also a woman, and share with her your feelings about being trapped in the cage of madi. Convince her that these rules are devoid of humane feelings. You are equal in status to your Mamiyar in that house. So why can't you bring about changes? You also have a responsibility and a duty towards the emotional development of your children..."

Girija came down rapidly from the ashram. The rain pelted down as she was about to engage an auto-rickshaw. So she changed her mind and got into a tempo parked by the side of the river. Though the tempo was protected by a tarpaulin, her sari got wet in the torrential downpour. The driver halted long enough to squeeze twelve passengers into the space meant for eight.. A newly-wed couple got in at the pharmaceutical factory stop. The bride was in a red zari[1] embroided sari, had painted nails, and wore sindoor in her parting. Husband and wife huddled together for warmth.

The bride's red handbag and the day's Hindi newspaper were wedged between her and Girija. The bold headlines caught her eye.

Fire aboard aircraft, Thursday...Flight from Bombay to Trivandrum. The rest of the news was blocked by the fold in the newspaper. Girija could think no further. She longed to ask for the paper but she could not bring herself to do so. Aircraft on fire....

He had said that he was flying from Bombay to Trivandrum. Was this a punishment for running away? What about her children.... Wasn't she their only support? For almost eighteen years she had walked in her husband's shadow, taken care of all his needs and borne him three children. Was she going to lose this bonding? Was she on the brink of a crisis? What was going to happen? Girija was in a trance till she reached Hari-ki-Pairi.

The rain had stopped. The sky was clear. She decided to continue her journey even though the bus had reached her stop.

---

[1] gold threadwork.

The couple alighted near the railway station. The newspaper slipped when the groom reached for his case. Girija hastily picked up the paper.

"Do you mind, I want to look up something in the paper. Can I see it for a minute?" She opened the paper without waiting for a reply. Below the photo of the plane, the news item read, "Five people sustained mild injuries. The fault was detected immediately after take off and the plane has returned safely to Bombay."

She returned the paper and said, "Thank you!"

"Keep it, Behenji."[1]

"No... I've had a look at it. I just wanted to read the headlines." Tension drained away like colours on a painting dipped in water.

For a short while, Girija had felt devastated. Where had her courage gone? Did not the movies exaggerate feelings of love, affection and bhakthi?[2] Was she irrevocably attached to Samu? No, that was not true. The day she married him, she had lost her freedom. She had been cooped up in a cage and her identity had been wiped out. But she was bound by ties of love to her children. If she had not had children she could walk away. Her care and concern for Samu stemmed from her affection towards her children.

57

With a light heart, she ordered tea at a roadside stall. It was not the kind of place she would normally have entered. It catered mainly to poor pilgrims and workmen. Huge freshly made puris were piled on a large plate. Milk for khoya bubbled in a vessel placed over a coal choola[3]. A boy in dirty clothes served puris and ladled the potato sabji floating in oil and chilli powder. If her Mamiyar could see her now!

"Chai, Mataji..." she turned around. The waiter handed her hot tea in a earthenware cup

"Kitna?" How much?

"Sat paise." She gave him the sixty paise and slowly sipped the sweet strong tea.

---

[1] sister.

[2] fervent religious devotion.

[3] coal stove.

She crossed the Ganga and spent the evening on the other bank of the river: The Ganga was transformed. The lamps began to float down the river giving it a festive look. She stood up.

"...Adiamma![1] where were you the whole day? The couple we met this morning spent a fortune offering pada puja[2] and bikshai to Swamigal. The lady asked me, 'Where is the girl who was with you?' I told them you were staying with us. When I asked her whether she knew you, she said that your face was very familiar. You had meanwhile disappeared and so she could not talk to you. And of course, you were not at the puja... Can you believe it, we discovered that my husband was distantly related to them. They are from my uncle's village Boodapadi and we traced our relationship through him. The man is my husband's maternal uncle's wife's brother's aunt's son. One would have imagined that they would be arrogant. But the wife went to great lengths to look after us. They have just left for Delhi by car because they are expecting a foreign guest this evening."

Gowri Ammal's fulsome praise of Roja Mami was unending. Her diamonds and silks, her car, her sweet talk and false smiles seemed to hypnotize everyone.

Gowri Ammal continued, "The lady said, 'We are leaving for the States tomorrow morning in connection with our son's marriage. Otherwise we would have been glad to have you to stay at our house.' They seem to have an unending stream of guests. She has given us her Delhi address and has extracted a promise that we will stay with her when we return."

Girija listened. What a relief to know that Roja Mami and her husband would not be there to taunt her...

All three had an early bath and a meal. Gowri Ammal dried her wet sari. They went to the market to buy pots filled with water from the Ganga, sindoor and the rolling pins for which the region is famous. Girija's knowledge of Hindi came in useful in striking a hard bargain.

"You have been like a daughter to us. We must have been related in our last birth. Aren't you returning with us?"

---

[1] an exclamatory expression equivalent of my good lady!

[2] the adoration of the feet of the guru.

Girija laughed.

"Yes Mami, I have exhausted five days leave..." She felt strong and relaxed. "We can take the night train which reaches Delhi in the morning. It will be easier to find our way home in daylight."

Since the old couple slept right through the journey, there was no time for any chit-chat.

THIRTEEN

"Mami, shall I drop you home?" "There is no need. You have already helped us enough. We have to catch the evening train tomorrow. Just put us in an auto-rickshaw and ask the driver to take us to Karolbagh. Our home is next to the milk booth on the main road".

Girija saw them settled into an auto-rickshaw.

"I hope you'll be alright...wait! I don't have your address.." panicked Gowri Ammal.

Girija was evasive. "We are moving house. Since I have your address Mami, I'll write to you. Who knows, I may even visit you."

"You are most welcome. God bless you."

Girija watched the auto as it took a U-turn and rapidly disappeared from view. The city was just coming to life. Children in school uniforms with flower like faces brightened the dusty brown pavements. Her children must have also left for school.

She got into a bus going to Madan Nagar. She felt strangely calm.

The bus took forty minutes to reach her sector with its familiar landmarks: pavement fruit stalls and fashionably dressed people around the expensive shops catering to the affluent..

As she got off the bus, she was greeted by Shivlal's son riding a scooter. "Namaste, Aunty, were you out of town?"

"Are you on your way to the factory?" she countered the question. Her tone was unruffled.

A group of poor children who attended the municipal school was about to cross the road. A voice piped up, "Aunty!"

It was Maya's son Dhanu. Normally he would not have called out to her. Her disappearance must have caused an upheaval at home. Sushma, in a pale blue salwar kameez, was on her way to college; a familiar face, a bright smile, a cheery "good morning". The street in which she lived wore its usual somnolent air. Two or three cars shrouded like ghosts were parked in each driveway. The owners' names were engraved behind glass on the gate posts. The corpulent owner of *Chandana* with her flabby white arms, sat in her doorway, eating breakfast. Girija had never paid much attention to her surroundings until now. Retired Brigadier Vikram Singh was watering his potted plants. Even though she had only a nodding acquaintance with him, his smile was friendly.

Sonu, the receptionist who lived across the road, ran out to ask, "Aunty, have you been away?"

"Oh! Yes." At last, she had reached home. The click, when she opened the gate, made Malhotra look up from his newspaper.

"Aayiye! Come! Where have you been? There's quite a crisis in your house."

Girija did not stop to reply. She climbed the stairs, two at a time. The front door was open. None of the children seemed to have gone to school. Bharath was the first to spot Girija.

He flung himself on her with a shriek of "Amma is back, Amma is back."

He asked innocently, "They told me you were a loose woman and that you would never return. Did you lose your way, Amma?"

The words lacerated her already wounded feelings. Hearing Bharat's voice, Samu, still in his striped pyjamas, came out, his face half shaven. She darted an angry look at him. "Who spoke such words to the child?"

Bharat chanted, "Amma has been found. We've got her back. She did not lose her way." Girija stood ruffling Bharath's hair. Her words dried up in the face of Samu's censuring look.

"Where have you been?" he asked.

"I went to Haridwar. Why did you use words with a double meaning to the child?"

"What else could I tell him? I told him you were a loose woman and had lost your way."

She had never heard him use that tone of voice before. It implied that since she had broken the rules, she would have to pay the price. Hearing her voice, Kavita and Charu came out from the kitchen. They had lost their sparkle. The oil and turmeric stains on Kavita's caftan were proof that she had been cooking. Charu had probably cut herself. There was a bandage on her finger.

"Hi Amma, Where did you go? Appa beat us, called us names and made us cook. Bunty's mother sent Tikku across to make chapathi and vegetables, one day. Patti created a scene and would not let him enter the kitchen. Ratna Akka came. Patti and Appa gave her a tongue lashing. I believe it was she who told you to run away. Appa and she had a dreadful quarrel." Charu recited her grievances like a child.

"Go inside, you donkeys! And as for you, Bharat, I am going to pack you off to boarding school. How dare she walk in coolly after four days as though nothing had happened! Haridwar, indeed! Whom are you trying to fool? Why did you go to Haridwar?"

"Listen, you have no right to talk like this in front of the children."

He took a menacing step forward as if to strike her.

"I'll break your teeth, you bitch! Who are you to talk about rights? You unchaste woman! I cannot show my face in public."

Patti looked out cautiously.

"Samu, don't! Let it not be said that we ill-treated her. Don't waste your breath. The milk is spilt and nothing can be done about it. Let her take her belongings and leave."

The witch!

Tongues of flame leapt up from the pit of Girija's stomach. Bharat was terrified and broke into sobs.

"Amma, will you go away again?" Samu pulled his son away. "Go inside, rascal, Amma indeed, who is Amma? A brazen hussy, a shameless woman! What an Amma!"

Patti intervened. "Samu, be quiet. You cannot eat a morsel of food, however tasty, once it has fallen on the dirty ground. Don't you remember how shaken the children were? Malhotra sent his son to search all the hospitals." Then she addressed Girija, "Why did you say you were going to the market? Why did you lie to me? I expected you to return any minute. When you didn't, I was chilled with fear. The children returned from school. Maya came, we combed the market for you. I did not know what to think. I did not know what to do. Samu was not in town. I phoned Roja. She came immediately and called up Samu. What could I tell him when he came tearing back? I said, 'She rang up someone in the morning. I asked whether she was ordering a gas cylinder, to which she did not reply.' Where could we search for you in this big city?"

"Were you bundled into a car gagged and bound like they show in the movies, Amma?"

The thirteen-year old girl's innocence was touching.

Samu raged, "Who would want to abduct her? She ran away of her own free will. She has been acting strangely of late, but I did not dream that she would be so bold... How dare you stand in front of me? You left the house four days ago for God alone knows what reason. You can now leave for the same reason. I neither know nor care where you were during the last four days. If you hadn't turned up, I might have continued searching for you. Now, I don't care where you have been, but you have brought disgrace upon us! I will lose face when I tell the Police Commissioner that you have returned. My reputation is ruined."

She felt as if someone had slapped her face.

What a heartless, savage attack! It was as if a jet of gas which she had forgotten to turn off was now ready to explode in her face. Life within these four walls was so fraught with danger that an unwary move could trigger off an electric shock. Why did her husband and his mother ignore her feelings? Why didn't they ask her what had motivated her to act as she did? Was she solely responsible for keeping the fragile bubble of family honour intact?

Unconsciously she must have spoken her thoughts, for he flared up, "What do you know about feelings? You lied to my mother and ran away when I was not around. You despicable woman! Why should we show you any kindness? I am not foolish enough to take you back. Since it has been my misfortune to have married you, I will make a settlement. My lawyer will get in touch with you.Do what you please. Don't come in the way of my children's future. I dare not show my face in this locality, because of you."

Roja Mami picked this moment to walk in. No one had heard the car arrive.

"So she has returned! I was so agitated that I kept calling Malhotra. He told me she had come fifteen minutes ago. So I rushed here."

Then, she had not left for the United States the day before. Girija was speechless.

Roja Mami turned to Girija. "Is this kind of behaviour right on your part, Giri? The children were in such a state! The old woman was inconsolable. She kept saying 'What can I do, Roja, she has brought us a bad name.' Charu telephoned everyone she could think of in an attempt to find you. Is this the way a mother behaves? That wretch Ratna turned up with two hulks and insulted Patti. Why should the old lady put up with such insolence at her age? Even at first glance, it was obvious Ratna was not our kind of person. But how could I tell you that? She and her gang smoke openly. As the mother of a sixteen year old, you should have quietly severed contact with her." She turned to Samu, "Don't misunderstand me Samu, but we have to guide our children. The girls have to be told to wear pavadai davani[1] on festival days. Samu, the reason I am saying all this is because these modern girls don't even wear kumkumam. There is nothing wrong in being forward. I too have visitors from all over the world, but do I give up my daily rituals or puja for them? The youngsters won't go to the Malai Mandir[2] on Tuesdays and Fridays unless you set them a good example. Will they respect our traditions if you criticize Patti's madi in their hearing? When you are out of town, Samu, your mother goes to bed hungry half the time."

Girija could not stomach it any longer. A wave of revulsion swept over her at the sight of this woman with her

---

[1] a two-piece outfit. An ankle length skirt with a half length sari covering the upper part of the body.
[2] the Murugan temple in New Delhi.

flashing diamonds, outsized pottu, dyed black hair and gaudy silks.

"Look here Mami, hold your tongue. How dare you interfere in a family's affairs and cause dissension? Tell me when you saw me starve Patti?"

Roja Mami said in a conciliatory tone, "Why are you so furious, Girija? I merely said that it is our duty to guide our children. We must instruct them to observe madi and celebrate Fridays in the auspicious months of Thai and Adi."

Girijia's self control snapped and she lashed out, "You sanctimonious hag! Your madi and vizhuppu[1] are all sham. You smuggle gold and diamonds, evade taxes and use an ignorant old woman's house to stash away your ill gotten gains. I don't want my children to become hypocrites, observing empty madi rituals."

Samu sprang forward and gave her a resounding slap on her face.

"How dare you? You bitch, you have the audacity to come back after keeping company with God knows who. Shut up!"

Giri's eyes flashed fire. "Look here, don't make false accusations. I did not run away with anyone. You dismissed all my years of servitude in an instant when you flung away your plate of food and walked out. Neither your mother nor Mami ever cared to take my side. I am not a mere wax doll. Over the years, you annihilated my self esteem and the life force within me. You made me work as a household drudge. The cruelty inflicted on me was worse than any physical abuse. Did you not ignore my role as the lynchpin of this household for eighteen years? I could not continue to function like a machine any longer. My power of endurance snapped. I went to the Ganga for solace. Roja Mami saw me there. Mami, why are you keeping quiet? You saw me when you came to offer bhikshai. How can you blatantly accuse me of such base behaviour?"

"What? I saw you! Where? Don't ask me to be a false witness. I have not seen you since I came here last."

Girija was stunned. Women seemed to enjoy destroying each other, instead of standing by each other.

---

[1] loss of madi.

"Mami, didn't you see me? You even established that you were related to Gowri Ammal. I went with her and her husband to Haridwar, stayed with them and returned with them this morning. You told Gowri Ammal that you were leaving for the States today to fix up your son's marriage. You apologised for not inviting her to stay with you in Delhi."

"Aiyo! What a tissue of lies! Samu, things have come to a point when we cannot be friends any longer. The bonds of love and friendship between our families are so strong that I looked upon your mother as mine and brought her all her favorite delicacies. Now what do I care? This is your house."

How could they allow Roja Mami to sever connections with them? Patti pleaded, "Roja, don't take it to heart. Right from the start, I was against having an educated working girl as my daughter-in-law. Girija's mother assured me that her daughter would never flaunt her education. For a time, she behaved herself. It is our misfortune that she has been brainwashed and led astray. The fault is mine for observing madi; if not for me, she could have done whatever she pleased."

"Amma, where is the question of allowing her to stay here after all that has happened? Don't blame yourself, Amma. I never thought that she was capable of such duplicity. Let her go where she pleases." Samu left the room abruptly.

How could Girija stay in this house any longer? She was forty-six years old, the mother of three children. Was it fair to tear a woman's reputation to shreds if she walked out on her family? Would any blame be attached to a man if he did the same thing? The family was an institution which legitimized the cruelty inflicted on a woman by her husband and his relatives. Only the man had inalienable rights. The woman had to break away from this structure if she wanted to reform it.

As Girija walked down the steps, Bharat followed her crying, "Amma, are you going away?" Kavitha chewed her fingernails. Charu, terrified of her father, stood apart, lips quivering.

"Hey, get inside, all of you. Bharat, come here. If you cry for your mother, you'll get nothing. Come on, I will buy you a remote controlled plane and a robot." Samu gripped Bharat's hand and cajoled him while Girija walked out with a resolute stride.

She did not look back.

FOURTEEN

Public telephones are unreliable at the best of times. Moreover, Girija had seldom used them. She went into the Post Office telephone booth. Coins in hand, she dialled the number of Ratna's University hostel. She got through after the fifth try. "Hello" said a male voice. She wanted to check whether it was the right number. "Yes, this is Abu speaking", she was reassured.

"Oh, I am Ratna's aunt Girija. Can I speak to her?"

"She has moved to the hostel in M.P. Road, very near your house."

"I need her help urgently. I have to meet her. Can you give me directions to get there by bus?"

"Sure. You have to take bus number 444 and ask for the Women's Hostel stop. I suppose you are ringing up from home?"

"No, from a public booth. I will return the completed questionnaire within the next four or five days. Can you call up Ratna and tell her that I am on my way? It is so difficult to get a connection from this booth."

"Sure. Tell me if you need anything else."

"I'll let you know. Thanks."

She replaced the receiver. The bus stop was not far away. She had taken only five hundred rupees in her handbag on that fateful day. Hardly anything was left of it. She had to count every paisa. She was once more the old Girija who would take an autorickshaw only when absolutely necessary.

She took the bus to the women's hostel which was a tall three-storeyed red building. The fourth storey was under construction. Ratna was on the second floor in room number two hundred and three.

When she knocked, the door was opened by a girl wearing a skirt and blouse, who was on the point of leaving.

The girl smiled. "Please come in. Abu called just now. Ratna is out and will be back by one o'clock. Please come in!" The warmth of her welcome assuaged Girija's sorrow. She felt as though she had stepped into the cool shade after being scorched by harsh sunlight. The girl offered her a glass of orange squash.

Girija was reminded of the old woman in Rishikesh. From the second floor window she had a distant view of lush greenery. As Girija finished the juice, the girl offered her another glass, which Girija accepted with a smile. The two-bedded room had a ceiling fan.

"Do you share this room with Ratna?", asked Girija.

"Yes, I am Annie." She said with a smile.

"I think you were just going out....."

"Yes, but make yourself comfortable. This door leads to the bathroom. I will tell the boy to bring you breakfast. Ratna will be back by lunch time. Here is the room key. Okay, see you." Annie left.

Girija relaxed. She closed her eyes and tried to erase the recent events from her memory.

In a traditional society, any woman who leaves her home is considered immoral. If she speaks to or associates with any man other than her husband, she is censured. However, the same yardstick is not applied to a man.

It was unthinkable that an educated woman who could earn her living had come to this state! Only in moments of stress does the truth come out. The value that Samu had placed on her was revealed in the moment of crisis. How could she be part of his family any longer?

But....Kavita, Charu......

When she heard a knock on the door, she suddenly became aware of her surroundings. She realised with a start that she had reached a new shore like the lamps on the Ganga. She got up to open the door to the boy who had brought breakfast. There was toast, jam, a boiled egg and a flask of coffee.

She freshened up in the bathroom and changed her sari. There was no arrangement for drying clothes. The room was reasonably tidy. A built-in steel cupboard was shared by the two occupants. The dressing table had a mirror in the centre with drawers on either side. Powder, nail polish and other cosmetics were placed in front of the mirror. A small writing table doubled as a dining table.

There was an earthenware pot with a clean stainless steel glass in a corner of the room. A soft cotton dhurrie[1] was spread between the two cots. Two pairs of bedroom slippers were placed under the beds. A few books were stacked on the window sill, which overlooked the verandah. Her eyes fell on a large shell with a heap of ash in it.. She shuddered. Obviously they were in the habit of smoking.

Perhaps there was truth in what Roja Mami said. In Girija's desperation to break free, what had she let herself in for?

To these people, did freedom mean being part of a permissive society where women smoked, drank and lived openly with men?

Thousands of questions swarmed around her.

Was the white object in the ashtray a cigarette stub? Perhaps! Even in wide open spaces the cool breeze carries dust.

She polished off the toast and coffee. She picked up a book and flipped through its pages. It was an anthology of poems and essays by Susan Griffith, published by the Women's Press.

She glanced at the titles.

Women-Motherhood-Woman-Religion.

Abortion-Sexual problems-Pornography.... Problems peculiar to the present generation were given prominence.

The author discussed the deep rooted problems in society from a feminist viewpoint and drew upon case studies to prove that the woman was always the victim.

In certain parts of America, where abortion was illegal, women who slept around and got pregnant described the difficulties of having an abortion.

She could not read further.

Something seemed to press heavily on her heart.

She could not digest the fact that in an advanced society a woman was degraded and looked upon as a mere sex object.

---

[1] a hand-woven carpet.

She was chilled with fear when she dwelt on the atrocities which were being perpetrated in this country, in this big city, on so-called liberated women behind the facade of civilized behaviour.

There was no clock in the room. Her watch had stopped. It was an old watch, a wedding present from her colleagues Rukmini and Bhagirathi. Was it not one o'clock yet?

A door banged. Ratna's voice could be heard.

She opened the door to Ratna who wore a stiff organdie sari and slung a bag on her shoulder.

"Hello!"

Ratna smilingly patted her on the back. "Abu's here. Shall we go down?"

They chatted on their way down.

Ratna had met Abu by chance in the library.

"Here he is, in the visitors' room. Relax, the two of you. I'll see whether we can get some lunch." Ratna disappeared.

Abu remarked, "Here's proof that there is no justice for an intelligent woman, if she is married to a man from an average family hidebound by tradition."

Girija responded, "This is an unforeseen development. I left for a quiet two days to think things over, away from my soul destroying daily routine. I needed breathing space from the back breaking work at home. If I had asked for their permission, it would have been refused. They did not even care to ask why I went to Haridwar. They spattered me with mud and threw me out..." Deeply moved, Abu asked after a pause, "Is your decision final?"

"I am confused..."

"I had a sister who was educated in Delhi and who enjoyed a lot of freedom. My parents got her married to a businessman in Nagapattinam who owned land, cattle and a house. She was five years older than me. The crime she committed was that she was better educated and more intelligent than her husband. My parents thought that she would be mistress of all that property. One day a terse message informed us that she had died of pox. She was only a fistful of ashes when we reached her house. I hope you understand my anguish."

"Couldn't you do anything?"

"What could I do? Don't we always look for rich husbands for our daughters? The boy's choice of a wife is made on the basis of the girl's beauty, wealth and her submissive temperament. Ratna is now working on a survey... Do you know which commodity in our country has the maximum export potential? .....Women—I hate to even utter the word 'body'! Ratna can tell you some shocking stories!"

"I have ordered chapati, vegetable and curd for both of you. Come to the dining hall," said Ratna.

"What about you, Ratna?"

"I have had lunch. What do you plan to do, Giri?"

Head bent, Girija traced a line on the floor with her toe. She did not reply.

"What happened this morning?" Ratna quizzed her.

Girija briefly recounted the events that had led to her leaving the house, stressing Roja Mami's part in the affair.

"Pooh! The raid is no secret. It was in all the newspapers. So, is Samu also involved?"

"I don't know. I am only worried about Kavita and Charu. I do not know how the mother and son will treat them. The reason for leaving the way I did was to chart out a bright future for my daughters. They should be educated and become self reliant. I have no faith in these posh schools and colleges. I am afraid..."

"Aren't you worried about your son, behenji?" Abu asked Girija with a smile.

"My husband and mother-in-law are very possessive about him. As I left the house, my husband was tempting him with a robot and a remote control plane so that he would put me out of his thoughts ." She continued, "They are not human. He will turn out to be like them."

"Don't let this turn you into a man-hater." Abu's tone was serious.

"Ratna, what I need most is a job and a place to stay. Samu will get a lawyer to sort out the legalities. I need my clothes and certificates. Can you help me? "

"Don't worry. We'll take care of everything. Take it easy for a week."

"I will, now that the boat has come ashore."

"Have your lunch."

Girija was being initiated into a totally new way of life.

Fifteen

Alighting from the bus in the evening rush hour was tough. Dust swirled over the sides of the roads, while the sun blazed overhead. Girija exchanged smiles with some of the noisy chattering girls who poured out of the bus and made their way into the hostel. Men were not allowed into the hostel and the rule applied to Abu also. Visitors had to wait in the visitors lounge downstairs. They could be invited into the dining room for a meal. It was not unusual for the hostel inmates to smoke and dress as they pleased. Ratna's room-mate Annie had been staying with relatives for the last ten days in order to accommodate Girija.

Girija's knees started to hurt even before she reached the second floor. She was out of breath. Runo, dressed in a long faded caftan, was coming down the stairs like a sleep walker. Her make up was blotched and she reeked of alcohol.

There were no raised eyebrows.

Giri let herself into her room with a key.

She looked at herself in the mirror. Her neck was bare, the gold chain was missing. In its place was a thin string of tiny red beads.

Her unadorned nose symbolised her new found freedom. She had removed her nose rings when she left home. She wore a small pair of earrings.

She took out a wad of notes from her handbag and counted it. One thousand five hundred rupees and a receipt from the bank.

She remembered the moment when Samu had placed the gold chain around her neck during the marriage ceremony at Thiruneermalai temple. Her entire savings had been used to have the gold chain made for her marriage. It was a symbol invested with great sanctity. For a long time, till Bharath's birth, she had worn her thali on a cord dipped in turmeric as well as the gold chain. At one point she had strung the thali on to the chain and done away with the cord—an act which had provoked much criticism from Roja Mami. However the gold chain had come in handy. She had pledged it to the bank to get some money.

Annie entered the room.

"Hello.... Did you go to Chittaranjan Park, Girija?"

"Yes. Reverend Mother asked me to report for work on the first. They can only give me a meagre salary of four hundred rupees now. Most of the school children are refugee children."

"Ha... take the job for the present. We went to your house to make sure your certificates and belongings are being despatched. Why did your mother-in-law weep so copiously?"

Girija had not expected this from her mother-in-law.

"The children were not at home and we met only your mother-in-law and Swaminathan. Our lawyer Prakash spoke on your behalf and explained that the divorce cannot be hurried. They have agreed to hand over your things.

"They did not say ....anything else..?"

"Why? Did you expect them to do a volte-face?" Annie laughed. Girija could not join in her laughter.

Why had Mamiyar wept?

Ratna took a look at her bare neck and patted her encouragingly. "Very good, Girija, you have taken a great stride forward. You have discarded some of our ugly customs. In a Tamil movie the title of which I forget, the heroine returns to her parent's house after a divorce. Her former lover next door is still pining for her. They decide to get married. The fellow says 'Remove that thing which your husband placed around your neck.' She cannot bring herself to take it off. She believes in its sanctity. She is in a dilemma. She dare not remove it. She changes her mind about remarriage. Even though she's divorced, her thali is still 'sacred' to her. How stupid! Girija... Shabash!" Ratna shook Girija's hand.

Girija wanted desperately to know if the heroine had two adolescent daughters.

"....Now, we must celebrate... Come.. Let's get some ice cream, Annie." Both of them vanished.

Barely five minutes after they left, a narmadi covered shaven head peeped into her room. And with her was Maya... Maya walked in carrying a suitcase... "Didiji?" She burst into loud sobs. Girija got up and pushed her chair towards Mamiyar. "Sit down Amma!"

"Why should I sit down? Your certificates and all your belongings are here. Check them.... I believe that marriage is like a perennial crop. It took you just one minute to abandon it.

"Did you have to take your husband's words spoken in anger seriously? All that he demanded was, 'What have you done for the family?' Were you ever denied anything? Were you ever short of money? Did we ever question how you spent it? Did we not buy you saris for Deepavali? Did you lack any comforts? A husband who willingly gives you his life has the right to lose his temper occasionally. A woman has to be submissive. That is what a family is all about. Patience enhances a woman's stature. At one stroke, you broke a relationship you enjoyed for eighteen years and cast a stain on our family honour. We can no longer show our faces outside the house. And we are saddled with two girls. Samu is worried sick at the thought of finding suitable husbands. At least that should have stopped you from behaving in an improper manner."

Girija's face turned red with anger.

"How can you accuse me of impropriety? It is you who spattered me with mud. What did I do to deserve it?"

"Haven't you done enough? Aspersions were cast even on a woman of impeccable virtue like Sita[1], although she came out unscathed from the ordeal by fire. But you did not care. You shrugged off your responsibilities and abandoned your family. After all, we are people with self respect."

"Did you come only to tell me this?"

Mamiyar said, "Check your things. All kinds of riffraff came to our house and harassed us. Ours was a respectable family, but not any more. He wants you to sign the list of all the things sent to you."

Girija opened the suitcase. Along with her certificates in a cardboard file, she found a cheque for ten thousand rupees. She looked at it with distaste.

---

[1] heroine of the *Ramayana*; a symbol of chastity, her character and conduct are questioned more than once.

"Is this a bone that you are throwing to a dog? Take it back!" She flung it away.

Mamiyar, alarmed by the tone of her voice, took a step backward. The cheque drifted towards her.

She swallowed her pride and walked out. Maya, wailing 'Didiji' followed her.

Girija sat staring into space.

Five minutes passed. Then ten... Everything was quiet.

Why hadn't Ratna and Annie returned with the ice cream yet? Where had they gone? Where were they?

Sixteen

G irija wandered aimlessly along the ve-randah and looked down. A crowd had gathered on the pavement in front of the hostel, all the cycles and scooters had come to a standstill.

An accident? Why was there a crowd inside the hostel also?

Fear gripped her.

An accident.... Ratna and Annie...?

She sprinted down the stairs after locking the room. On the staircase she saw girls in small groups, heard snatches of conversation in English and Hindi, anguished murmurs.

"Kya hua? Kaun?" What happened? Who is it?

"It is Runo! She jumped from the second floor."

Runo? She had met her on the stairs to the third floor only a short while ago. Runo.... hardly twenty... a child-like face.... She worked as a receptionist...

Why had she jumped down? Drugs? Had she been in full possession of her faculties?

Her heart wept, "Andavane[1], Andavane!" Annie and Ratna must be in the crowd. She went in search of them.

Annie was nowhere to be seen. Ratna, towering over the others, was trying to push the crowd back.

---

[1] Tamil for O Lord!

Two girls were administering first aid to Runo who was lying face down.

The police and an ambulance arrived. Ratna spotted Giri and ran towards her.

"Giri.. it's unfortunate... We may be late returning. No hope... She may not survive.."

"We feel dreadful! She is from an affluent family. She has no mother. Her father is a third-rate chap and a drunkard to boot. She was a neglected child. Her father brought home a mistress. Runo found herself a boyfriend and got into bad ways. He had come this morning. A lot of people saw them together."

Giri said, "I saw her too. She was rushing down the stairs."

"Isn't it terrible! By the by, I saw your husband in his car sometime ago. Did Mamiyar come upstairs?"

"Yes, she brought all my things."

"Okay, I'm going now, take some rest." Ratna rushed away.

Long after the body was removed, the hostel girls huddled together and discussed Runo.

Seventeen

The sentence had pierced Girija like a nail.

"She has no mother. The father is a drunkard who brought a woman home."

Her Kavita...Kavita... She had come of age... She had never learnt to obey.

Now they would discipline her. They would incarcerate her in the kitchen and make her follow madi rules. She would be under strict surveillance on her way to and from college.

Kumaraparuvam, adolescence, is a difficult stage. The children in Kavita's school were spoilt brats from wealthy families.

She could not shake off these thoughts....

She drifted unawares into sleep. Somebody banged on the door. She was unable to get up and open it. She felt as if she were bound hand and foot.

Giri...Girija, wake up, open the door... Kavi...Kavita... had an accident with the geyser in the bathroom...She's been electrocuted. Get up...Aiyo...Aiyo ... Kavita..!

A knot tightened in the pit of her stomach... She screamed. Her eyelids were glued together. How would she get up and open the door?

"Giri...? Giri...?"

They broke open the door. Ratna...it was Ratna.

Aiyo! Why did I let myself be swayed by them?

Kavita, Kaviyamma, I've never allowed her near the gas stove. The plug of the geyser must have been defective. Appa and Patti would not have noticed... A geyser is a luxury... Who wants it?.. Kavi...Kavi!

Ratna pushed open the door. "Giri, Girija! What happened to you?"

She splashed water on Giri's face...

At this point Girija woke up with a jolt.

Ratna asked in concern, "What's the matter Giri? Is there anything wrong?"

"What's happened to Kavita? How is my child?"

"There is nothing wrong with Kavita. She must have gone to school. Did you have a bad dream?"

Ratna looked exhausted. She must have had a sleepless night.

"We are waiting for the post mortem report. Annie is with Runo's brother who is inconsolable. It's unfortunate! Obsession with love makes one a coward. Runo became a drug addict. When her boy friend ditched her, she ended her life. On the one hand your Mamiyar, with her madi rules and on the other, Runo with no rules."

Ratna placed her hands on her head.

"Che!"

Girija looked intently at Ratna for a while, then got up to brush her teeth and wash her face.

She ordered the boy to bring two cups of hot tea.

"Giri, I think the incident has disturbed you deeply."

"Y...yes.. But I will not go back to them like a dog with its tail between its legs. I will not beg for forgiveness. Only if I live like you in the outside world can I prevent other Runos from taking shape."

"Oh Giri! Didn't Mamiyar ask you to let bygones be bygones and to go back?"

"The question never arose. I would have relented for the sake of the children if she had asked me to go back and if the man in the car had wanted to meet me. But... he arrogantly deputed his mother to remind me that after all I was only a woman and that my actions were unpardonable. As proof of his magnanimity, he sent me a cheque for ten thousand rupees.I flung the cheque away."

Ratna said nothing.

"Mamiyar brought my certificates and clothes. However, I had left my jewels there."

Giri urged Ratna, "Go and have a wash. Tea is ready."

Girija made her bed and swept the room.

It was probably past seven o'clock. Groups of children were on their way to school.

A girl as fat as Kavita walked past in a blue and white uniform.

She kept staring. The sharp edge of her dream had hurt her. What was to prevent Kavita from becoming another Runo? The elements were there — Kumaraparuvam, the awkward adolescent stage, strict household, indoctrination that her mother was evil.

"Giri, why the faraway look? The tea is getting cold." Giri came away from the window and began to sip her tea. Ratna took out a packet from her handbag. Sandalwood powder.. fragrant sandalwood powder. She placed a sandalwood cone in the shell shaped dish. She rolled a piece of paper tightly, set a match to it, and then lit the cone. A thin wisp of smoke curled upward like a snake.

"Can you smell the sandalwood, Giri?" Ratna closed the window.

The fragrance did not pervade the room, even if you inhaled slowly.

"We have been cheated with adulterated stuff. We bought it when we were on our way to get ice cream the other day.We heard that someone had leapt out of a window of the women's hostel, so we rushed back. We had to spend the whole night between the hospital and the police station. Che! This sandalwood has no smell." Ratna was frustrated.

"Ratna, when I saw a heap of ash in this ashtray, I thought you smoked. I mistook the roll of paper for a cigarette stub. At the back of my mind was Roja Mami's accusation that you and people like you smoked."

"Roja Mami is capable of saying anything. Now she will accuse you of giving in to the same habit. She will claim that there are enough grounds to ostracize you. I suppose it is true in a way. We see all types in this hostel. Girls like Runo, who lack mental maturity are quite common—suicide is their way out. It is sheer escapism. The likes of Roja Mami often read pornographic novels on the sly and drink at parties. Women who observe acharam also avidly read cheap Tamil books and watch titillating movies. Have you ever wondered why, Giri?"

Ratna went on. "In a way they are also victims of some form of repression. They cannot be their natural selves. So, they delude themselves into believing that those who do not practise madi, acharam and religion are obsessed with the gratification of their senses."

Giri listened intently.

"Normally, people don't realise that freedom and culture go hand in hand with knowledge. Giri, we are not against anybody. But we women have to fight those forces within society which do not allow us to be ourselves. Ever since we began to think for ourselves, these forces have begun to oppress us even more brutally. I feel that the male species was not so cruel in the past."

Girija's mental processes, so long dormant, came to sudden life.

"Ratna, I feel unhappy when I think of Kavi and Charu. They need to be in contact with me. They should grow up to be free, mature human beings. I may be cast out from the family, but I cannot let go of them."

Tears blurred her vision.

Ratna held her hand comfortingly.

"I agree with you. Certainly our struggle is just about to begin."

The sandalwood cone was reduced to a mere heap of ashes. Ratna opened the window wide.

....

Rajam Krishnan:
Her writings and background

We discern two trends since the 40s and 50s in the Tamil literary scene while examining the engagement of literature with social issues. The need for social amelioration was felt urgently and was visualized in terms of the Gandhian ideals by one group of writers. There was a stress on moral integrity, ethical purity, and idealization of the common man and village life. Industrial and technological advancements were viewed as antithetical to life which was close to nature which Gandhiji extolled. Writers like K.S. Venkataramani, Kalki, Akilan, Na Parthasarathy belong to this school. The other group took a distinctly Marxist turn and projected class conflict as the central focus. The bourgeois feudal society was severely castigated. Raghunathan (*Panjum Pasium*), D. Selvaraj (*Malarum Sarugam, Theneer, Mooladaram*) Chinnappa Bharati (*Thagam, Sangam*), Ponneelan (*Karisal*) may be cited as examples of those who voiced their views from the Marxist angle. Together these two groups may be regarded as pioneers of social realism.

It is in this context that we must place the writings of Rajam Krishnan. She started as a novelist with Gandhian leanings. Her early works *Kurinji Then* and *Verukku Nir* provide instances of her way of thinking in this period. The fist novel is a chronicle of the tribal life of the Badagas of the Nilgiri Hills. The author examines the changing phase of the community in a span of sixty years. The transition meant a deep division in the people between old values such as growing only food crops and sharing everything and leading a peaceful life, and the new values which meant cash crops and market economy, which made people self-centred and money-oriented. The Gandhian thought is expressed in a subtle way with the author betraying a nostalgia for a lost way of life based on love and peace. In *Verukku Nir* the author openly denounces the degeneration of values in post-Independence India and criticizes the upsurge of violence all over. She stresses the need for a revival of Gandhian principles.

The appeal of Marxist principles soon took hold of Rajam Krishnan's creative impulse. She called for a radical reform of society. In fact she developed in her fiction the distinctive method of concentrating on various groups of the most oppressed communities and classes in our society. Her *Karippu Manigal* exposed the difficulties of those who worked in salt pans. *Setril Manithargal* focussed on the travails of the peasants; the fisherfolk and their sufferings in life are the theme of *Alaivai Karaiyil*. Child labour is condemned in *Koottu Kunjugal* which depicts the plight of the innumerable children working in the match factories in Sivakasi down South.

Thus socio-economic exploitation has been the consuming concern of the generation of writers since Independence. The theme of oppression inevitably has led to a focus on the present generation, especially on one of the prominent targets in all classes and communities: women. The emergence of women's writings and feminist writings is best understood historically in this context. If we turn to the English speaking world we find a similar situation. Class oppression subsumed gender and even race oppression in the colonial countries and even in the United States. Women writers started protesting against sexual discrimination and social obliteration. In fact the influence of Marxism on the Feminist movement itself is the marked feature in Britain. It accounted for the emergence of Socialist feminists in the 50s.

In the Tamil literary scene also the alliance of Marxist and Feminist thinking is quite discernible. Common to both is the pressing need for questioning the existing state of affairs and offering a revaluation of history with reference to the treatment of women. We have radicalists who question the staple features of patriarchal social organization. Ambai and Sivagami belong to this class. Before their emergence we have the rare introspctive writing of Chudamani. It is marked by a finesse in rendering the interiority of female consciousness. Chudamani is however neither as socially conscious as Rajam Krishnan is nor rebellious like Ambai. Writers like Ambai have an additional distinction of altering the very idiom and narrative mode in a subversive way to demolish the establishment. As such their reading public tends to be trained readers, sometimes even a coterie. They would prefer not to write for a popular medium. On the other hand we have women writers like Rajam Krishnan who have not only straddled both the older and younger generations but have synthesized the lasting traditional values with the best in the modern developments in social organization. They have imbibed the best in feminist ideology recognizing its justness. Further they have the humanist perspective in view while championing the cause of women. Rajam Krishnan's forte is to encompass the whole of society and not focus on the psychological upheaval in the individual alone, in fictionally transmuting the feminist values. A further point of distinction about Rajam Krishnan as a woman writer as distinguished from the radical feminists, is her capaacity to hold the interest of the elistist as well as the Common Reader (to use Verginia Woolf's apt term). Those who are unacquainted with the feminist ideology and terminology are nevertheless able to respond with enthusiasm to Rajam Krishnan's projection of the predicament of women in our society and they acknowlede the justness of her castigation of the wrongs in it.

Rajam Krishnan: A profile

Rajam Krishnan's career as a writer has been prolific. This woman writer who is about 70 years of age, has had a remarkably productive career since she began with her first novel *Swathanthra Jothi* (1948). Since then she has never looked back, publishing almost continuously. Especially during the period 1983–1992 she has about 18 works to her credit, sometimes two or three coming out in a year. They include a full-length biography of the poet Mahakavi Subramanya Bharathi, treatises and chronicles on women such as *Kalam Thorum Pen,* a primer for youngsters *Gandhi Darisanam,* a biographical novel about a woman revolutionary *Pathaiyil Padintha Adigal,* a study of feminism since Vedic times *Kalam Thorum Penmai,* besides social novels such as *Suzhalil Mithakkum Deepangal* and *Manidathu Makaranthangal.*

Her interests in society are wide-ranging although we may be justified in saying that her central concern now is the treatment of women in Indian society. The purposiveness of Rajam Krishnan's writings is clear when we note that she has a deep historical sense of our complex culture and a deep conviction about the value of our social institutions. She is constantly led to compare the ideal/ideology with the reality that obtains. Hence she does not render any issue in skeletal or abstract terms. In *Mannagathu Poonthuligal*, for example, the tragic woman protagonist bemoans the time when marriage was mutually respected by both the parties and there was fairness in the demands made on the girl's family. The degeneration has set in, the author believes, in the last 50 years or so. She wants to set the perspective right.

Ultimately she wants to set society right. It is this aspiration which gives an urgency to the purposiveness of her fiction. There have been artists committed to ideologies in all cultures. Generally 'committed literature' turns out to be propaganda and therefore discursive. Whereas Rajam Krishnan's commitment is to nothing less than establishing a society on the principles of enlightened/rational spirituality, humane interaction, mutual respect and sense of responsibility as a citizen.

Since her output is voluminous and covers well over a period of 45 years, it is impossible to give an account of all the novels and works she has published. Hence what is offered here is a brief resumé, done genrewise, of some of her achievements.

Documentary Fiction: The special feature of Rajam Krishnan's writings is her concern for social reality as she perceives it. It has impelled her to undertake a thorough research in the area of the social problem that she wishes to explore in a given work. Every reviewer and commentator has remarked on her meticulous study of the relevant region, its people, its dialect, idiolect, its register, its values and customs which constitute an authentic matrix. Each of such studies would make an academic social scientist acknowledge its throughness. She is keen on relating her 'sense of the past' (as Eliot would say) to the contemporary state of the society. Hence the bias in her writings to expose the distortions of values inherited from the past and the burning desire to set them right. In American and British literature we have a sub-genre called the documentary novel or non-fiction novel — which is a fictionalization of journalistically researched material (e.g., Joseph Heller's *Catch 22*). Rajam Krishnan's penchant for field work before putting her writings in semi-fictional forms brings her closer to this new journalism. As in Heller she uses this talent for a relentless satire of the predatory impulses of individuals and institutions in her society. *Kurinji Then* is one of her best in the early phase. Her novel *Manikka Gangai* (1986) on the tea-estate workers repatriated from Sri Lanka, or her examination of female infanticide in the novel *Mannagathu Poonthuligal,* is an example of her range of interests and her method of exploration. Her novel *Mullum Malarum* is a testament of non-violencee and it deals with the Chambal Valley decoits. *Valai Karam* has for its theme the Goa liberation movement. Some of her documentary novels are based on real life events, as for e.g. *Alaivai-Karaiyil* which deals with the life of the fishing community.

Novels of Social Realism: Rajam Krishnan writes with effortless ease novels which depict the life of men and women in our society. The situation of a man who is spurned both by his wife and mother because he transgressed the Brahminical codes of conduct is presented in *Vilangugal. Suzhalil Mithakkum Deepangal* on the contrary portrays the struggle of a young woman in an orthodox Brahmin family to find her self and come out of its stultifying routines and not to submit to its patriarchal demands. It boldly projects her search for spiritual clarification on the banks of the Ganga and her resolution at the end to be a 'new woman'.

Social Treatises: The orientation to research in Rajam Krishnan finds yet another expression in the form of trenchant treatises, particularly in the field of feminism. *Kalam Thorum Pen* (1989) is a study of the portraits of women through the ages since the Vedic period. Like the most recent American New Historicists she examines the ideology behind the 'representations' of women. She makes bold to question even some of the canonical texts in Tamil like *Thirukkural* for indirectly putting women under patriarchal subjection in the name of an ideal wife. This spirit of undaunted criticism is a mark of Rajam Krishnan's writings; she never fears any sectarian force which reigns at a given moment and holds power in its hands. She castigates the present-day society for sugar-coating the bitter pill with ancient ideals to lure women into subjection. One is reminded of John Stuart Mill's urbane tract "The Subjection of Women" in the Victorian period in England which highlighted the need for restoring women's status through education. Rajam Krishnan's subsequent work *Kalam Thorum Penmai* (1990) is a sequel to the earlier work. The title indicates the shift of interest from giving an historical account of women portrayed down the ages to the ideology of modern feminism and its implications for Indian women in the present time.

Biography: Rajam Krishnan's contributions to well researched biography fills a lacuna in Tamil writings, as one reviewer notes. Her biography of a famous doctor in Madras, Dr. Rangachari who was also a philanthropist, is a very good instance in point. It is hailed as a substantial contribution to the genre in Tamil. The title of her biography of the nationally known Tamil poet Subramanya Bharati reflects her feminist slant. It is a paeon for a poet who hailed womanhood by singing the praise of Draupadi in his poem "Panchali Sabatham". It is a full length biography running to 640 pages. She has also written a biography of a revolutionary woman called Maniamma who was a nationalist, and who turned a disillusioned Communist but ever remained a true sympathizer of the proletariat cause. It is a bold variation on regular biography (See her book *Pathayil Pathintha Adigal*). For it is cast in the form of a biographical novel. The book serves several interests at one stroke. It extols the courage of conviction of a woman in the early years of the nationalist movement to defy the taboos of an orthodox society (she being a widow) and venture into humanitarian acts such as helping the oppressed farmers in the heartland of feudalism, Thanjavur. She dressed herself in men's clothes and was a Gandhian by conviction. Rajam Krishnan has attempted to add narrative interest to her chronicle of this courageous woman.

Children's Literature: The range of Rajam Krishnan's prose includes the simple narrative which appeals to children. She has a few children's novels to her credit: *Kakkani* (1983), *Ikkini Arasakumari* (1986), *Ammavum Thozhargalum* (1988). Her essays on Gandhian philosophy *Gandhi Darisanam* (1986) may be mentioned here since they are meant to initiate children into the ideology of Mahatma Gandhi.

Travelogue: Rajam Krishnan has also attempted writing a travelogue. Her *Natpuravin Azhaippu* 1987) gathers her impression of her visit to the Soviet Union. Mention may also be made of her novel *Annaiyar Bhoomi* which is on the Soviet women.

Translations

a) She has some significant translations to her credit. She has translated from Malayalam to Tamil *Kazhniya Kalam* (1980), an autobiography by Sri. K.P.K. Menon. Roy Chaudhri's *Folk Tales of Bihar* has been translated from English to Tamil. Rahul Sankritya's *Manava Samaj* has been translated from Hindi to Tamil.

b) Her reputation as a prominent novelist has been so high even outside of Tamil Nadu that some of her works have been translated into other languages like Malayalam and Hindi (e.g., *Verukku Nir, Setril Manithargal, Karippu Manigal*) and Gujarati *(Verukku Nir)*.

Published creative works

1. Swathanthra Jothi	Novel	1948
2. Penn Kural	Novel	1953
3. Anbukkadal	Novel	1955
4. Mayach Chuzhal	Novel	1957
5. Malai Aruvi	Novel	1958
6. Banuvin Kadalan	Novel	1958
7. Kaivilakku	Novel	1958
8. Sivappu Roza	Short stories collection	1959
9. Nithya Mallikai	Short stories collection	1959
10. Pachaikkodi	Short stories collection	1960
11. Alli	Short stories collection	1960
12. Oosium Unarvum	Prize winners short stories collection	1960

13. Kurinchithen	Novel	1963
14. Dr. Rangachari	Biography	1965
15. Nizharkolam	Novel	1966
16. Amudamaki Varuka	Novel	1966
17. Kurunjir Pookal	Novel	1967
18. Alaikadalile	Short stories collection	1968
19. Valaikkaram	Novel	1969
20. Solaikili	Novel	1969
21. Vidiyumun	Novel	1969
22. Kattukkaval	Short Novel Collection	1969
23. Thangamuth	Novel	1970
24. Puyalin Maiyyam	Novel	1971
25. Pavithra	Short Novels	1971
26. Iruthiyum Thodakkamum	Short Novels	1971
27. Venukkunir	Novel	1972
28. Roja Idazhkal	Novel	1973
29. Malarkal	Novel	1974
30. Mullum Malardidadu	Novel	1974
31. koodukal	Novel	1975
32. Vilankukal	Novel	1975
33. Annaiyar Bhoomi	Novel	1976
34. Chalanankal	Novel	1976
35. Veedu	Novel	1977
36. Alaivaikaraiyle	Novel	1978
37. Pudyageetham Isaikiran	Essays	1978
38. Uyirppu	Short stories	1978
39. Karippu Manikal	Novel	1979
40. Vadikal	Short Novel	1979
41. Koottukkunjukal	Novel	1980
42. Manithanum Jothiyum	Short Novel	1980
43. Osaikal Adanghipiraku	Novel	1982
44. Chetril Manitharkal	Novel	1982
45. Panchali Sapatham Padiya Bharati	Biography	1983
46. Kakani (for youngster)	Novel	1983
47. Manudathin Makaranthangal	Novel	1984
48. Bharatha Kumarikal	Short Novel	1984

49. Pudiya Chirakukal	Novel	1985
50. Ikkini Rajakumari (for youngsters)	Novel	1985
51. Kalam	Short story collection	1985
52. Manicha-Gangai	Short story collection	1986
53. Gandhi Tharisanam	Essays	1986
54. Oomai Aranngal	Novel	1987
55. Nadppuravin Azhaippu	Travelogue	1987
56. Sulalil Mithakkum Dweepangal	Novel	1987
57. Mannakathu Poonthulikal	Novel	1988
58. Annkalodu Pennkalum	Novel	1988
59. Thottakkari	Novel	1988
60. Ammavum Thozharkalum (for children)	Novel	1988
61. Kaalam Thorum Pen	Sociological study on Indian women	1989
62. Oomai Arangal	Novel	1989
63. Thottakkari	Novel	1989
64. Kanavu	Short story	1990
65. Kalanthorum Penmai	Social Research	1990
66. Azukku	Novel	1990
67. Paadiyil Pathintha Adigal	Novel	1991
68. Mayilampattu Valli	Novel	1992
69. Aval	Short story	1992

Prize winning works

1. *Oosium Unarvum*
   Best short story in Tamil—International short story competition held by New York Tribune—1950.
2. *Pennkural*
   Kalaimagal Narayanaswamy Iyer Prize for the year 1953.
3. *Malarkal* Ananda Vikatan Novel competition First Prize 1958.
4. *Verukkuneer* Sahitya Academy Award for the year 1973.
5. *Valaikkaram* Soviel Land Nehru Award for the year 1975.
6. *Karippu Manigal* Ilakya Chintanai Award for the year 1980.

7. *Chetril Manithargal* Ilakya Chintanai Award for the year 1983.
8. *Chetril Manithargal* Bharatiya Basha Parishad (Calcutta) Award for 1986–87.
9. *Blind Child* Kalaimagal Silver Jubilee Award for drama.
10. *Chuzhalil Midakkum Deepangal* Tamil Valarchi Kazhagam 1989.